Remarkable Restraint

ISBN # 978-1-78651-368-7

©Copyright Devon Rhodes 2016

Cover Art by Posh Gosh ©Copyright 2016

Interior text design by Claire Siemaszkiewicz

Pride Publishing

Published in 2016 by Pride Publishing, Newland House, The Point, Weaver Road, Lincoln, LN6 3QN, United Kingdom.

Books by Devon Rhodes

Vampires & Mages & Weres Oh My!

A Pint Light
Through the Red Door
Locke, Stock and Barrel

International Men of Sports

A Sticky Wicket in Bollywood
Chasing the King of the Mountains
At First Touch
Blindsided
Burning Up the Ice
Serving Love at Carnival
A Grand Prix Romance
An Ace in the Tiebreak

Grad School Guys

Remarkable Restraint
Naughty By Night

Homecoming

A Detour Home

Feral

Pride and Joey

Anthologies

Unconventional at Best

REMARKABLE RESTRAINT

DEVON RHODES

Dedication

For Ava March — you know why!

Chapter One

Chaz Warren groaned with frustration as he removed his hand from his cock and gave up his fruitless quest for orgasm...yet again.

Two months, he thought with mingled disbelief and pride, turning over onto his stomach on his bed. The comforter abraded his tender flesh in a beguiling way, but he resisted the urge to thrust. He knew from experience that it was useless to try to get off that way and it would just serve to exacerbate his arousal. The thick black plug in his ass shifted as he moved, and he pushed backwards with his hips and bit his lower lip until it settled.

It wasn't even noon yet, and a light sheen of sweat covered his naked body, the ceiling fan doing little to combat the brutal August heat wave. It had been hard to get to sleep, then he'd ended up oversleeping. He must have had a sexy dream he didn't remember, because his morning wood had been almost painful. So after he was done in the bathroom, he'd decided to have a little fun.

He swiped at a trickle of sweat running down his neck then ran his hands over his head, alternately tugging his short blond hair and scratching his scalp. He was still weary, having been unable to sleep well all week knowing that Justin would be back any day now. He was actually supposed to have been back four days ago, but according to the fuzzy message Justin had left on his voicemail, some road had washed out in flooding and put the bus behind schedule, so he and some other guys had missed their original flight. He hadn't heard from him since, and the waiting was driving him crazy.

Warring emotions were tying his stomach in knots. Chaz was nearly dizzy with excitement at the prospect of finally seeing the man he had secretly been in love with for years—and been with almost daily just as long—after the summer-long separation. But he was uncertain how Justin would feel about him after two long months with their only contact being a few hurried phone calls and voicemails. At this point, he hadn't spoken to him in weeks, which made his mind go to unpleasant places, especially given the emotional state of confusion they had parted in in the aftermath of the farewell party in June.

Chaz and his best friend and roommate Justin Travers had spent that warm, early summer weekend at the beach at a friend's beach house party, blowing off the built-up stress of getting through the spring semester of their master's program and finals. It had been a sort of combination end of term party for a couple of friends and a send-off for Justin, who was heading away for the summer to do volunteer work before returning to continue his master's degree work in the fall.

Chaz hadn't even wanted to go to the beach house. Though he knew the group of guys who was going to be there, they were more Justin's friends than his. He didn't really feel a part of the group, and the partying atmosphere wasn't his scene. But Justin, in his usual forceful style, had bullied and nagged him into it, and in the end, had simply taken matters into his own hands, literally herding Chaz into the car. It was the story of their long friendship—Justin deciding for the two of them and Chaz inevitably trailing in his wake.

The Twins, their mutual friends called them—completely ironic, considering that they didn't have a single feature in common. Justin, with his dark, riotous curls over sapphire blue eyes, was the polar opposite of Chaz, who had close-cut straight blond hair, plain brown eyes and pale, occasionally freckled skin. But you never saw one without the other, at least until this summer. Chaz shook his head and flipped onto his back again, stifling a gasp as the breeze from the ceiling fan caressed the taut, overheated skin of his shaft like a physical touch.

Giving up any pretense of trying to get some sleep in the suffocating warmth of the bedroom, Chaz rose and walked toward the kitchen of the apartment he and Justin had shared. Officially, Justin still lived there, even though he had been gone all summer, volunteering at a worksite in Central America. His bedroom held all his belongings — he hadn't bothered to pack up, declaring that he'd rather continue to pay his half of the rent than store everything. That had been fine with Chaz, who had been dreading the thought of interviewing potential new roommates. The thought of living with anyone else besides Justin, even just for a summer, gave him a strange, sickening feeling inside.

Chaz glanced by unconscious habit into Justin's quiet and tidy room as he passed the open doorway, then stopped short, his gaze sharpening as something caught his eye in the dim light cast from his own room. A package lay squarely in the middle of the bed — an item that he knew for certain hadn't been there earlier today.

He walked slowly into the room, looking around. Nothing else was different. He knew this room as well as his own, and some nights, he could only get to sleep on Justin's bed. He never got under the covers — somehow it seemed less an invasion of privacy if he stayed on top of the sheets, carefully smoothing the covers back into place each morning. Chaz tried not to examine his motivations for doing this too closely, telling himself that Justin's room wasn't as uncomfortably warm as his own.

Yeah, right, he mocked silently.

The padded envelope, which was identical to another package that had sent his heartbeat soaring two months earlier, had his name on the front — *Charlie* — in Justin's slanted scrawl. Justin was the only person who ever called him that, and he secretly loved that Justin called him by a special name. He could almost hear the deep, resonant, slightly scolding tone jump off the paper.

No postage or address — this had been hand-delivered...

He tore into it, needing to see. His pulse sped up as he stood rooted to the spot, staring at the shredded strips of T-shirt and the swimsuit that he knew he hadn't seen since the beach trip with Justin. Since that crazy, mixed-up night that had changed everything...

Chapter Two

Two months earlier

"Travers! Your serve, man. Heads up!"

His teammate's shout finally drew his attention away from the beach house atop the cliff and just in time, too. Justin barely caught the volleyball that Kellen lobbed at him across the sand before it hit him in the chest.

"Pay attention. I don't want to have to buy the beer tonight," Cody muttered as Justin passed him on the way back to the service line.

"Yeah, yeah." But Justin did try to pull his head back into the game and he narrowed his eyes against the sun, which was getting low to the horizon. Kellen, Byron and Avery all looked ready to pounce all over whatever he threw down. The three guys on the other side of the net had been practically joined at the hip since they were kids, and thus had teamwork perfected. They were hard to compete against.

But then again, he had Simon and Cody on his team, and they were no slouches either, especially Cody, who'd played college basketball as an undergrad. Cody's roommate Simon wasn't overtly athletic and didn't have a killer instinct, but he made up for it with amazing accuracy with angles. Not surprising from the tall, summa cum laude engineering major.

As though magnetized, his gaze went back to the beach house. Still no sign of Charlie. Justin sighed. The sooner they got this game done, the sooner he could go up and see what the hell his roommate was doing when he should be down here having fun on the beach and celebrating the end of term.

He gave the volleyball a high toss with his left hand then jumped and brought his right around overhead to slam the serve across the net. Byron was able to get a piece of it, but it went flying well out of bounds and gave Justin, Cody and Simon match point.

"Damn it!" Byron yelled. "Come on—where the hell did that come from?"

"Just saving the best for last," Justin responded as Avery jogged to get the ball then passed it to Simon.

"Yeah! Now that's what I'm talking about." Simon ran over to pound Justin on the back and hand him the ball.

"One more point and these guys have to do the shopping for tonight," Cody chimed in, sounding relieved. Justin knew the future doctor of veterinarian medicine was particularly strapped for cash as he'd had no family support while going through college. Now in his fifth year, he was working two jobs and studying his ass off to keep his grades up to maintain his scholarships.

Avery rejoined his roommates on the other side of the net and they all put their heads together for a hurried conference. The Dog House boys, they were known as, because of the long-time name of the place close to campus they rented. The family who owned it had built a huge, modern house pretty much right in front of the old farmstead on the big lot. There was a narrow driveway down one property line back to the Dog House—so called because it was so small and sat behind the bigger house on the property…just like a dog house.

"Strategize all you want," Cody called out to the best friends. "This match is ours."

Justin glanced up at their rental for the weekend, hoping for a glimpse of his own best friend, but no dice. Their opponents looked like they were ready again, though Kellen and Avery had switched places, hovering toward the baseline. Byron was still in the middle, close to the net, and gave Justin a challenging grin, likely just waiting for a shallow serve he could poach and smash back across to their side. No surprise that he was Justin's biggest competition, as they both shaded toward the dominant side of the BDSM spectrum, much more so than their friends, who were mostly vanilla, though there were a couple of guys Justin would be willing to bet were somewhat submissive.

And then there was Charlie. Nothing 'somewhat' about *his* leanings…

He immediately cut off that line of thought before he popped wood in his swim trunks.

Before the guys could heckle him any more for taking too much time, he tossed the ball up and sent a blistering serve across the net. It was too high for Byron to get a hand on this time and headed into the back court. Kellen and Avery both dove at the ball and Justin could see what was going to happen a second before they collided, knocking heads then collapsing to the sand. "Oh fuck."

The game forgotten, all of the guys converged on the two downed players. Justin got there last, and was relieved when both guys sat up with assistance, holding their heads. Everyone knelt in the sand around them.

"Are you guys okay?" Simon asked.

Avery groaned, resting his arms on his knees then his forehead on his arms.

Kellen gave his crown one last rub. "You're not going to throw up, are you?" Kellen asked Avery, sounding more worried about his friend than hurt. He patted Avery's shoulder.

"Fuck, no—leave me alone. God—one time when I was twelve and you think every single time I get hurt I'm going to hurl." Avery lifted his head and squinted. There was a definite lump just above his temple. "Man, you have a hard head."

"I'll go get you some ice," Byron offered.

Justin jumped to his feet. "I'll come too."

Byron smirked but didn't say anything until they were

out of earshot of the others. "Are you that skeptical that I can manage to get ice by myself? Or maybe there's another reason you want to go up to the house."

Justin shot him a look but couldn't deny it. Byron was the only person who knew about his long-standing — and unrequited — feelings for his best friend. Feelings that weren't just brotherly, or even just romantic. Justin had suspected for a long time that Charlie was not only gay but likely submissive. However, even now that they were postgraduates, Charlie still hadn't come out, even to him. He didn't date, though Justin had a strong feeling that he might have done some stuff with their neighbor, Andy, who gave both Charlie and Justin knowing looks at times.

He'd tried to broach the subject with Charlie every which way without actually coming straight out and asking him, but it was either ignored or went over Charlie's head. Which wouldn't be surprising. Charlie sort of lived in his own little world sometimes. It brought out the caretaker in Justin — always had.

He let Byron precede him onto the narrow staircase up the bluff to the house. "If you're talking about Charlie, it's true, I haven't seen much of him since we got here. And soon I'll be gone for the summer." He followed Byron, admitting, "That'll be the longest we'll have gone without seeing each other since we became friends."

They'd met and become instant best friends when Justin had moved during high school, and had continued their friendship through college by rooming together. Justin casually dated — it always felt like cheating to him, so he kept things short and simple. He mostly dated women since he tended to compare all men to Charlie and came up lacking. At the club, he was more likely to choose a male sub for the evening, but while he'd developed experience as a Dominant, he hadn't taken on any sub on a permanent basis. That, again, just hit a bit too close to home.

There was only one guy he could imagine in his life long term in any respect — one man he had strong feelings for —

and it was as if Charlie had no perception of Justin in that light.

Bryon stopped with his hand on the doorknob. "It's your own damn fault for not following your instincts years ago."

Justin sighed. "I know." He'd let Charlie's silence on the matter go on too long and now there was a yawning chasm between them that seemed to be growing wider by the day. Something about their friendship had taken a turn over the past few months. He could sense Charlie withdrawing, holding himself back from Justin in a way that he couldn't pinpoint but definitely felt the effects of.

But Justin had a plan. The timing sucked with his summer already committed to volunteer work out of the country, but last week, to his utter relief, he'd finally found the proof he needed that Charlie might be not only open to, but welcoming of, Justin's bent.

During finals week, he'd asked to borrow one of Charlie's suitcases for the trip. With his head buried in a textbook, Charlie had absently given him the okay to grab it from his room. But when he'd gotten it to his bedroom, he'd found that the case was locked. Rather than disturb Charlie again, he'd gone ahead and rummaged through his desk drawers then the top of his dresser before trying his nightstand, looking for the little suitcase key.

Justin could vow with a clear conscience that he really hadn't started out snooping, not consciously, but as soon as he'd opened the second drawer down, he'd frozen. There, peeking out from under a pad of paper, had been all the proof he wanted that some future might be possible between him and Charlie. He'd pulled the top magazine out, noting that there were at least half a dozen below it. He hadn't had to look through it — it was obvious from the cover and topics that it was geared toward gay men...who were into the same lifestyle as Justin.

"I wanted him to trust me and tell me himself," he added to Byron as they gained the top of the long flight of steps, who gave him a sympathetic nod.

15

He had done a bit more surreptitious poking around then, even as he'd bemoaned the fact that he'd be leaving so soon and for so long. He'd found no sex toys or condoms, nothing more than some lube tucked in the very back of the top drawer. That had immediately sparked an urge to add some fun items to the drawer to see Charlie's reaction. The idea that had followed he'd already put into effect, though Charlie wasn't yet aware. Justin was planning on talking to him while they were here, in the privacy of their room in the evenings. Last night, though, he'd chickened out, struck with uncharacteristic self-doubt.

What if the reason Charlie hadn't confided in him was because he simply wasn't interested? Added to that, it seemed as though he was withdrawing — pulling away from Justin — and that was something he couldn't let happen.

Byron opened the back door. "I'll take the ice down to Avery. I think I can manage that myself if you want to..." He gestured to where they could just see the top of Charlie's head above the couch then gave Justin a wink and headed into the kitchen.

Time was marching on, and soon he'd be in Guatemala for two months. He had to make a move tonight, make the most of the next two days...then let the time apart hopefully work in his favor.

Chapter Three

Chaz heard the door and stopped reading for a moment. Was someone coming in or leaving?

"Hey, Charlie, let's go for a swim before dark."

Justin flopped down next to Chaz on the couch and, as always, Chaz warmed at his friend's presence.

"You already have your trunks on," Justin continued. "C'mon, man, let's head out."

Chaz didn't bother to look away from the paperback he was now pretending to read while shaking his head in response.

"Didn't you get enough of reading while you were studying?" Justin tried to grab the book, but Chaz anticipated him and quickly moved the book away from his friend's hand, knowing that if Justin got hold of it, he'd likely never see it again. Justin lunged for the book again, landing across his chest with a grunt, using his hand on Chaz's shoulder for leverage.

The bulky weight of Justin's six foot two of sheer muscle pressed Chaz into the couch. "Hey!" Chaz complained, shoving ineffectively at the large man. Although he had worked out religiously since high school, he had never managed to add much more than definition to his wiry five-foot-nine-inch frame. Justin had at least forty pounds on him, and he felt every one right now.

"Why are you up here bugging me, anyway?" He tried to squirm out from under Justin, avoiding eye contact as he tucked his book into the cushions of the couch for protection. "I thought you were down playing volleyball with everyone."

Justin relented finally and sat up, leaning back next to Chaz, so close that he could feel the heat of Justin's arm radiating against his own, their knees brushing. "I don't know if you've noticed, but it's almost sunset." Justin sighed. "I've hardly seen you since we got here. You're always reading or going off on walks by yourself." A touch of hurt surfaced in his voice. "I'm leaving in two days and I'm gonna be gone for months. I...just want to spend some time with you. Okay?"

Chastened, Chaz swallowed, his heart dropping at the reminder of how little time they had left. He turned his head and stopped breathing, shocked at how close Justin's face was to his own. He was caught by those brilliant blue eyes, the dark lashes as long as a girl's. Justin's dark, wavy hair was always just a little too long, but it suited him—carefree and wild, a force of nature. Chaz dropped his eyes to those full, luscious lips and felt a familiar stirring deep inside as his cock abruptly twitched to life.

Justin rolled his eyes as Chaz got up, pointedly protecting his book, and walked around the table to sit on the other sofa.

"I don't know why you even came," he groused.

Chaz burst into laughter at that. Justin scowled at first then was forced to give in to a wide grin. Chaz's heart beat a little faster. As always, he was pleased at seeing those lips stretched in a smile, proud of his ability to keep Justin entertained.

"Okay, and why are we laughing at me this time?" Justin was killing him, lounging carelessly on the couch opposite his, those long, tanned legs stretched out in front of him. He cocked his eyebrow in inquiry, another sexy little quirk that made Chaz's chest ache.

Chaz shook his head in wonder. "You don't know why I came? Like I had a choice!"

"What do you mean?" Justin got up and pressed his linked hands toward the ceiling, then stepped across the table and dropped next to Chaz again.

Rolling his eyes, Chaz stifled a sigh. Trying to keep his distance from Justin was an exercise in futility sometimes. The man had no concept of personal space, especially for a straight guy.

He gave a snort and opened his book again. "When was the last time you *didn't* make me come along on whatever you had planned?"

"I didn't make you come!" Justin nudged his arm then tried again to grab his book.

Chaz lifted up briefly and sat squarely on it. "You packed my bag. You pulled me out to the car in my bare feet, for crying out loud. Hey!" Justin reached between his legs in an attempt to get the book, and accidently thrust his inner wrist along his half-hard cock, tweaking his balls in the process. His body went on red alert having Justin's hand anywhere near his penis, and the burgeoning erection took on embarrassing proportions.

His eyes widened in panic. He pushed free and stood abruptly, only to have Justin seize his waist and pull him back down onto his lap, clamping his arms around him in a bear hug to negate any resistance he might have offered. He nearly moaned as the amazing sensation of being restrained by Justin lit up every button he possessed, and he began to struggle in earnest, needing to get away before his best friend noticed his straining erection and discovered his closely guarded secret.

"Charlie," came the harsh whisper in his ear. "Stop."

He froze instinctively at the command in that compelling tone, barely breathing as he felt Justin's lips brush across the sensitive hollow below his ear, rubbing back and forth, catching slightly on his skin, mimicking a kiss. He could feel a hard ridge nestled snugly into the valley of his ass, and his mind raced as the implications of that wholly unexpected observation finally occurred to him.

"Justin?" he began shakily, but then they both froze at the approach of loud, boisterous voices as the rest of the group began making their way up from the beach.

19

With only moments before the first head would appear at the top of the stairs to the large back deck, Justin spoke quietly in his ear. "Our room—go there and wait for me." He released Chaz, giving a firm boost that propelled him toward the staircase.

Chaz staggered for a couple of steps before catching his balance, then quickly moved toward the stairs up to the sleeping areas. The top floor of the house was divided into a small bedroom with two double beds and a huge loft with a mish-mash of various beds and futons. Through some leverage that Chaz was unaware of, but not terribly surprised by, Justin had managed to secure the privacy of the bedroom for the two of them, leaving the bigger communal room to the rest of the guys.

He hurried into the room, closing the door behind him, his mind racing at the unexpected turn of events. He had lusted after Justin from afar since the first day of high school, when the tall, athletic kid assigned to the same locker had turned out to be as nice as he was good-looking. Like a light bulb coming on, Chaz had realized that very day that his indifference to girls wasn't the result of being a late bloomer, because he was anything but indifferent to his charismatic, and very male, locker mate.

His internal acknowledgment that he was gay was equally momentous and mundane. Momentous because his fantasies and wet dreams from that moment on took flight and featured strong, masculine hands forcing him to his knees, firm erections jousting with his—mundane because there wasn't a single opportunity to act on any of these desires in reality, so publicly coming out wasn't really necessary.

He had eagerly anticipated college as the time when he would be able to be sexually open and free, a new man. But his personality stubbornly remained more shy and studious than wild and crazy, and so the extent of his 'hands-on' experience with the same sex consisted of occasional brief encounters with his closest friend besides Justin, their adorable and outrageous neighbor, Andy. Even those friendly exchanges were few and far between, in the very short intervals between Andy's constant parade of hot, buff boyfriends. So Chaz was still technically in the closet—not from shame or fear, but mostly just due to lack of a sex life altogether.

A couple of years ago, he had discovered the eye-opening world of gay BDSM erotica and magazines—and eventually porn—which turned the vague and inexperienced longings inside him into a burning need that he could finally put a name to. A dizzying variety of scenes now played through his head during his solitary play time...but the partner in his mind's eye never varied. It was always the strong form and mesmerizing voice of his best friend, Justin.

Lately, these graphic images, combined with the natural way that Justin seemed to steer and control his life, had made his infatuation almost impossible to conceal. He was alternately dreading and needing Justin's absence this summer. The constant imaginings made for a fantastic fantasy life, but Chaz couldn't dare to dream that his sexy, masculine friend would ever return his interest, which was heartbreaking to consciously admit. Justin had dated girls all through high school and college, never being serious or exclusive, but a steady diet of them just the same, and he had certainly never given any indication of gay or bi leanings.

It was probably just the wrestling around that caused Justin to spring wood.

He came to that conclusion and winced as he tugged down on his tight sac, trying to will his erection away before he had to face his roommate.

* * * *

The back door opened and the cluster of guys came tromping in. Avery held a baggie of melting ice to his temple, and Justin could tell that Kellen was trying hard not to hover.

He and Byron agreed that Kellen had it bad for his friend, but they had no idea what could be keeping them apart. Byron had surmised that it was possible that Kellen didn't want to go there and risk messing up their long friendship. If that was the case, Justin could relate.

"I still say that serve was long," Byron was saying to Cody.

"No way. The spot where these two collided was well in bounds. Dinner's on you guys."

"Seriously? You're going to make poor Ave go to the store like this?" Kellen gestured to his friend.

Cody's brow puckered. "Ah…crap. I guess not."

"Let's just order some pizza. We still have enough beer and soda for tonight," Simon suggested. "I'll kick some money in for me and Code." Cody opened his mouth to argue and Simon jumped in, "Hey, I still owe you gas money for driving over."

Those two started a quiet argument while Avery and Kellen started looking through the papers by the house phone, evidently searching for a takeout menu.

Byron flicked a glance at the now empty couch then arched an eyebrow at Justin. "What happened with Chaz?" he whispered.

Still riding high from Charlie's promising response to his overtures on the couch, Justin really wasn't in the mood to hang around and let his momentum fade by acting like a teenaged girl gossiping with Byron, or debating over pizza and the volleyball match with the Dog House guys. "Not much yet. Cover my part—I'll give you some cash later," he said softly to Byron then strode toward the stairs.

"Good luck, man."

Justin gave a nod before he disappeared around the corner. He needed all the help he could get. Swallowing against his nerves as he climbed the staircase, he tried to think only positive thoughts, because he was determined to make this work.

One way or another, before this weekend came to an end, he was going to find out what was bothering Charlie, fix it somehow then confess how he felt about him and hope that Charlie felt the same.

Chapter Four

Chaz felt a trickle of sweat down his back and pulled his shirt off. He sat down on the closest bed — Justin's — and took a deep, steadying breath. Sharing a room with Justin this weekend had been an exercise in frustration. He'd found himself watching covertly as his friend unabashedly changed clothes in plain view, revealing his mouthwatering body, the tanned, rippling muscles of his chest and abs bare of hair except for a dark treasure trail leading into the nest surrounding his magnificent thick cock. Chaz made excuses to leave the room whenever it wouldn't be too obvious that he was running away. All that intimacy was hard enough to take with the unrequited love and lust he felt.

Then last night had come the disconcerting and unmistakable sounds of Justin stroking himself off.

Chaz groaned aloud at the memory. At first he hadn't believed what he was hearing, but a slow, stealthy turn of his head to the left had him gaping and panting without sound as he was able to put the visual of Justin's hand rhythmically moving beneath the sheet together with the audible murmurs and groans. Chaz had shifted as quietly as he could, wishing Justin would lose the sheet, trapping his erection with ruthless pressure between his thighs as he lay still and silent. He'd watched in an agony of need until Justin had come with a stifled gasp, then turned onto his side toward Chaz. With his friend facing in his direction, but no way of telling in the dark whether his eyes were open, Chaz had had no choice but to grit his teeth and bear his painful arousal until he'd finally fallen into a restless sleep.

The sound of the door opening had him springing to his feet in embarrassment at being caught on Justin's bed, holding his discarded shirt in front of his erection like a shield. He met Justin's burning stare and shivered with want at the intensity he read there.

Oh God, he is so fucking sexy.

He had an errant, fearful thought and pinched his arm, wincing at the sting.

Nope, not a dream.

Justin closed the door behind him and deliberately flipped the lock, holding Chaz prisoner with his gaze as he approached, stopping only when they were almost chest to chest. The differences in their height put Chaz nearly eye level with those full, sensuous lips, and he swallowed hard as his body swayed forward instinctively, tipping his head up, trying to connect with that sexy mouth. He watched Justin's jaw clench, and he caught himself just in time.

What are you doing, dumbass? He's straight as an arrow. He's just as likely to deck you as kiss you back. Probably even more likely.

Bitterly aware that he was probably misinterpreting his roommate's actions over the past half hour, he took a step backward to give himself some space. His heart began hammering in his chest as Justin followed with a step of his own, bringing them back to kissing distance, crowding into Chaz's space in a deliberate and confident manner that had Chaz repressing a shudder as he felt a drop of pre-cum dampen his swim suit lining.

"Charlie. It's time for you to stop avoiding me and just tell me what the hell is going on with you."

Charlie took one last look into Justin's fascinating blue eyes and found that he couldn't continue to meet that demanding gaze, so he dropped his focus again to those lush lips, the ones that had inspired so many shower-time fantasies in the past. He stifled a groan — that wasn't much better for his control — and settled on Justin's chin as neutral ground.

"Hey, hey, it's okay. I'm not mad—I'm just concerned."

Justin's hands came up to run along his arms before taking them in a firm grasp, and that was when Chaz realized that he was shaking. The feel of those strong hands clamping his arms down sent him dangerously close to the edge, and he knew he had to get away *right now*. He wrenched his shoulders, dropping his shirt, and almost gained his freedom before Justin recovered from his momentary shock and, with a sigh of exasperation, threw him face down onto the bed, keeping him in place by straddling his thighs and pressing his wrists to the mattress with barely any effort.

"Stop it, Charlie! Just stop. What the hell? Why do you keep acting like you're afraid of me all of a sudden?"

Chaz went still at his first word, trying to catch his breath, his mind roiling with confusion. *I'm such an ass.* Justin probably wasn't even aware that Chaz had felt his erection downstairs. Hell, he probably hadn't even realized he had had one. It seemed like his roommate went around half hard all the time anyway, from what Chaz had seen over the years. And he had freaked out and overreacted, attributing more to it than there was. No wonder Justin was confused by his idiotic behavior.

"That's it," Justin stated. "I'm sick and tired of you avoiding me. We are going to stay right here like this until you tell me why you've been ducking me."

The warm weight of his friend just below his ass conjured up a whole new host of images that tightened Chaz's cock to the point of cramping his stomach muscles, his balls pulling up. He could feel himself on the brink of coming, and knew he had to get Justin off his back—both literally and figuratively.

"Answer me."

Another involuntary shudder worked its way up his frame, and he found himself responding. "It's nothing," he snapped. "I haven't been avoiding you. I'm just tired and not interested in all the jock shit you guys do. And I'm *not* afraid of you. You're my best friend, asshole."

26

Justin's eyes crinkled at the corners. "Thank God—there you are. I wondered where you went. But why do I feel like you're lying to me?"

Chaz sighed and ducked the question. "I don't know why you've gotten this in your head. Jesus, man. Let me up already. You're too fucking heavy."

"Nope."

"What?"

"You heard me. Until I get an answer I can believe, you're staying right here." Conversely, his arms were released at that moment, but just as he braced his hands on the mattress to push himself up, he heard, "Stay."

"What am I, a fucking dog?" A motion rocked him into the mattress, Justin moving from his thighs to square on his ass. That shift in pressure in turn pressed his erection into the mattress and made him temporarily forget to try for freedom as he closed his eyes to fight to keep from coming. An odd ripping sound had his eyes flying open again. Glancing back over his shoulder, his mouth gaped at the sight of Justin without a shirt, muscles bunching as he tore his T-shirt into strips.

Huh?

"What the—? What are you doing?"

Quicker than Chaz could react, Justin shifted his weight from Chaz's ass to the small of his back and grabbed his right wrist, tying a strip of the ruined shirt around it then skillfully securing it to the headboard.

"What the *hell*? Justin?"

Chaz finally remembered to struggle, but by then, Justin was securing his other wrist as well. He tugged in vain, but although the bindings weren't tight enough to cause pain, they were fastened well.

Justin began to rise. As soon as the weight left his back, Chaz got his knees under him, crawling toward the headboard to try to get some slack that he could hopefully work with to get free.

"No way, Charlie." A pause. "Fine. Legs too, then."

Firm, warm hands manacled his ankles and pulled him back flat on the bed. He tried twisting to the side, but the only thing he accomplished was getting his stiff cock caught in a painful downward bend as Justin ruthlessly restrained his ankles, his legs spread wide to each corner post of the footboard. He didn't even have enough slack to raise his foot more than a couple of inches, and the slack on his wrists was completely gone, the fabric pulling with pressure where his wrists met his hands—not uncomfortable exactly, but he was definitely at Justin's mercy.

Oh, get real, Charles Warren – this is fucking hot.

It was the stuff of fantasies, and he knew that he would be reliving this scene with his hand on his dick for the rest of his life.

Still, gotta get him to let me go before I come.

"Justin?"

No answer. He squirmed a little, the uncomfortable position making his cock twinge in a painful but perversely pleasurable way. Wanton images sprang into his head of cock rings, leather straps...

He swallowed and tried again, craning his head back awkwardly to try to see his roommate's face. "Justin? This is really uncomfortable. Please let me up, and I promise we'll talk. Okay?"

That now familiar ripping sound again then fingertips brushed lightly across his temples, smoothing his hair back, soothing him, before a wide strip of the shirt snugly blindfolded him.

"There. I don't want you hurting yourself trying to watch me. We have a lot to talk about, so I want you comfortable, because I have a feeling we're going to be here a while."

Be here a while? Comfortable?

That brought the plight of his bent erection back to mind, but Chaz would be damned if he'd ask for help there. He tried to surreptitiously wriggle enough to free it, but the inner lining of his swim trunks had gotten twisted and out of place during their struggles, and he only succeeded in causing some heart-stopping friction. He could feel the leg opening bisecting his balls so that one was outside the mesh.

Chaz also became increasingly aware that his ass was well on display and squirming around would only bring attention to it. He wondered where Justin was and what he was looking at.

If I didn't have the swimsuit on...

He moaned aloud this time. If the shorts weren't on, his hole would be completely vulnerable to Justin's gaze, his legs spread as widely as they were.

Vulnerable to his gaze, his touch, his tongue...

"Uh," he panted, not at all certain he would be able to hold back if Justin touched him now. It was delicious torture, not knowing where he was, what he was doing. He gave another tug at the bindings. Caught. His heart hammered in his chest as he began to panic.

"Justin? Please let me up now. I'm begging you. Please. Justin? Oh God, please let me up. I can't...."

"Shhh. Relax." Soothing, but nonetheless a firm command. A warm, comforting hand was smoothed down his bare back. "I'm not going to hurt you, okay? I never would — you know that. But we need to have this out."

Chaz quieted by degrees, finally submitting as the tension drained away. It was true that he had complete faith that Justin wouldn't harm him. Accepting that Justin was serious, but would let him free as soon as he was satisfied, he gave a nod.

"Good. Now, Charlie, I'm going to straighten you out, and then we're going to talk."

Straighten me out?

Chaz was bewildered until he felt a masculine hand slide up his inner thigh and inside the leg of his shorts.

Oh God. Holy fuck.

He felt pre-cum welling and a flash of pain as his tortured cock pulsed in warning.

Don't come, don't come, don't come...

The hand brushed lightly over the taut, sensitive skin of his wayward balls before gently arranging them back inside the mesh inner lining. He instinctively rocked, trying to push further into the hand cupping his sac, then stopped, mortified. All the while, his shaft was hard as a rock. He couldn't help another breathy groan as he fought to keep from pressing down again and trapping Justin's hand beneath him. He canted his hips to try to escape the overwhelming touch, but this only resulted in elevating his ass in the air, as if in invitation.

The hand pulled out from under him. "There—comfy now?"

He remained as still as he could, fighting for control. Then, there was a new problem for his waning control to deal with—a firm hand came down hard on his ass.

Oh yeah…

Chapter Five

"When I ask you a question, I want an answer. Comfy?"

Chaz was stunned and completely aroused by this side of his best friend's personality. "Uh..." Another smack had his balls climbing as if trying to burrow into his body. "Comfy...no," he managed.

"Ties too tight?"

"No," he answered without thinking then backpedaled. "I mean, yes. Please untie me."

"I don't think so. Now tell me what's bothering you before I really paddle your ass."

Wow.

Before *that* image could derail him by taking hold in his overheated imagination, he snarked back, "What could be bothering me? Oh, you mean besides the fact I'm tied to the bed by my surprisingly sadistic roommate?"

That earned him a growl and a third hard blow to his now-burning right ass cheek.

"Jesus, man," his wayward mouth ran away from him, "if you have to do this, at least hit the other side too."

A huffing laugh. "Thanks for the suggestion." And Justin rained down a trio of sharp blows, alternating sides this time.

Chaz was extremely glad for the barrier of the shorts he still wore as he breathed and shuddered through the pain, but felt like his balls were seriously going to explode if he didn't get his cock free and come soon.

"Last time. What do you need?" Justin stroked his hand gently over his rear, soothing the sting.

Your cock up my ass. "I'm, uh, crooked."

"Crooked?"

"Yeah, you know, my…uh…"

Justin moved his touch along his hip and slid underneath Chaz, barely coming into contact with his straining dick before he changed direction, slipping his hand inside the waistband of his trunks, unerringly finding his hot erection and cradling it in a gentle grip.

"That can't feel good. Do you want me to fix it?"

Chaz could only nod, breathless with the effort of trying to remain indifferent to the intimate touch.

"Ask me then."

Chaz's cheeks burned, and he was at once glad for the blindfold. "Yes, I want you to fix it."

A hard swat from Justin's free hand drove his hips down, crushing his erection into the hand cupping it. Chaz winced as more pre-cum leaked out. Right into Justin's hand. *Shit.* Chaz had no idea how his straight roommate was not totally freaking out by now with someone else's cum in his hand.

Straight, but apparently kinky and Dominant, a gleeful little voice whispered in his head, prompting another spurt.

"That wasn't asking. That was telling. Now, Charlie" — he caressed his stinging ass again — "ask me."

"Justin." He swallowed. "Will you please help me?"

"Help you with what?"

"Jesus…"

"Be specific." Justin lifted his hand from his backside as if preparing for another blow, and the fingers around his cock flexed.

Chaz stammered in his haste to comply. "Pl-please straighten out my dick, Justin. I mean, will you please? Um, will you please fix it? Oh God, Justin…" His voice rose on this last plea as the hand holding his erection gave one last squeeze before straightening the shaft to point it up in a more natural direction toward his belly, giving one long, firm stroke with his open palm as if to smooth it into place.

Like a garden hose with a kink that was suddenly removed, he was helpless to stop the eruption that finally had a conduit to travel — and travel it did, harder and faster than he had ever come in his life. All the mental and physical stimulation of the scene was finally too much for Chaz to bear, and he gave a loud cry as he jammed his hips into the warm mattress underneath, pinning Justin's hand in place as he came in wave after wave of utter, unbelievable pleasure.

Justin, Justin. Oh God, Chaz thought in a dizzying blend of embarrassment and elation as he spent himself into his roommate's hand.

What have I done?

Chaz lay boneless and confused in the quiet aftermath, glad again for the blindfold that kept him from chancing meeting Justin's eyes. He imagined the disgusted expression his roommate must be wearing. He winced. Or maybe disappointment? Pity?

It wasn't exactly the way he had planned to come out to his best friend, and he braced himself, wincing again as Justin finally removed his cum-sticky hand from inside his trunks.

He heard Justin moving around, a rustling sound, then the bed shifted as he settled between Chaz's legs, running his dry hand gently along his bare back while pressing his legs even farther outward with his knees.

Chaz's mind was mush, but even in his sleepy, spent state, he recognized the position he was in. "If this is what you wanted to do, you should've taken my shorts off before you tied my legs," he finished around a jaw-breaking yawn.

He both heard and felt Justin's chuckle as the blindfold was whisked away. Chaz blinked and raised his head, turning it enough to glance behind him. Justin was sitting back on his heels between his legs, his own legs spread, and he was rhythmically stroking his beautiful, erect cock with the hand that...

Oh God, he's getting himself off with my cum!

Chaz's over-stimulated shaft gave a feeble twitch of interest.

Justin wore a slight smile as he gazed down at him and Chaz warmed with pleasure. He was going to have enough memories from the past hour to fuel his fantasies until he was too old to do anything about it.

And even then, this will probably do the trick.

The smile on Justin's face dropped and his sapphire eyes burned into Chaz's as an intense expression pulled his handsome features taut. His rhythm faltered then sped up, and Chaz felt the heat of his cum splash in pulse after pulse on his bare skin.

"You're mine, Charlie…" Justin groaned as he marked him with his seed, then he collapsed onto Chaz's back, his chest smearing his cooling cum between them.

Chaz dropped his head back to the bed and closed his eyes, replete, the image of Justin coming on him burned into his brain. He could feel the waning erection nestled against his ass, the welcome weight of his beloved friend on top of him. For a moment, he pretended that they were together and this could be his forever. Almost immediately, his mind started punishing him for that impossibility.

It's called getting off, idiot. It has nothing to do with you.

But he said I was his.

Yeah, well, so he's naturally Dominant and a little kinky. And apparently bi. That doesn't mean he's suddenly in love with you!

Silence reigned. He cleared his throat. "Can you please untie me now?"

Lips brushed his neck as Justin countered, "Why have you been avoiding me?"

He didn't see the point of not answering the question anymore, not after what had just happened. Not with Justin lying on top of him and his cum covering his back. "I want you, okay? I always have. I'm gay, and I wanted my best friend…who I thought was straight up until a couple of minutes ago. It was just easier to deal with when I started keeping my distance." That wasn't exactly the truth—it hadn't made it easier, but at least he hadn't had to worry so much about betraying his secret.

"And that's why you've been acting strangely around me? And you didn't tell me this, why? Jesus, Chaz, I thought we were best friends."

Chaz, not Charlie? We were best...? Oh no...

"Justin—" he began, but stopped as Justin lifted himself up and knelt over him. The lack of expression on his usually happy-go-lucky friend's face was too much to bear, and he dropped his head again as emotion began to prickle at the back of his throat.

Chapter Six

Justin's heart thrilled to Charlie's words about wanting him, even as he fought disappointment that he hadn't thought he could confide in Justin. So much time had gone by – time where they might have been able to be together for real if one of them had had the guts to speak up. He kicked himself for not manning up and making his interest known, but Charlie had hidden his interest well.

He ran his possessive gaze down Charlie's pale back where the smears of Justin's cum were starting to dry. A pleasing sight but time to let him go. Justin struggled to undo the tight knots binding Chaz's wrists, leaving the strips attached to the frame, then moved to the foot of the bed and untied his feet.

Chaz was free, yet, perversely, he didn't move.

Justin stood, tucked himself back into his swim trunks and sighed. "C'mon, man, upsie daisy."

He manhandled Charlie around into a sitting position on the edge of the bed, which exposed his cum-soaked swimsuit. Chaz flushed and dropped his hands into his lap as though for camouflage.

"Seriously? Now you're shy about it?" Justin teased, trying to get back to his usual demeanor. "I know you got off. You came in my hand, remember?"

Charlie turned as red as Justin had ever seen him, and he worried that his face might explode. He kept his eyes down and head hanging, and Justin got the impression that Charlie was silently willing him to just leave already.

Not going to happen. Time's too short as it is.

Justin dropped down between his legs, resting his hands

on Charlie's knees, trying to reassure him with a casual, undemanding touch. Charlie raised his hands to his head, rubbing his scalp and tugging at his hair in the unconscious way he had done ever since Justin had known him whenever he needed comfort.

"You and your hair," Justin observed wryly. He squeezed Charlie's knees once before he pushed off and stood up, walking aimlessly across the room. "I've known you were gay since high school, Charlie," he confessed. "That's never bothered me. I always wished you would tell me yourself, though." He ran his hand through his hair, sighed once more and looked at Chaz, who was watching him with a sad expression that he couldn't quite decipher. The silence stretched between them.

"I'm sorry," Charlie blurted finally. The desperation in his voice made Justin's breath catch. "I just want to be friends like we always have. It won't ever happen again."

Justin had begun shaking his head before Charlie had finished talking. No way could they go back to tiptoeing around each other like they had been. Now that Justin had had a taste of what they could be like, going back sounded like the worst idea ever — and impossible, at least on his part.

Charlie was looking more and more panicked, as though he was about to bolt, and Justin knew that he had to take charge of the situation.

"Coming without my permission? No, it won't."

Charlie's jaw dropped and his face reflected his shock. "What?"

Justin watched him carefully as he spoke, "The timing on this sucks, and that's my fault." Charlie started to protest, and Justin cut him off with a gesture. "I'm the one who forced the issue. I was planning to wait until I got back from my trip for the majority of this."

"For what?" Chaz had no idea where this was heading and was trying his hardest to fight the little bubble of hope that was welling up inside him.

"To bring you into the scene."

"Scene?"

Justin looked at once amused and irritated. "You scare me sometimes with how freaking naïve you can be. After everything that happened tonight, after all the magazines you keep in your bedside table and all the e-books on your Kindle, you really don't know what I mean?"

Chaz turned beet red at the thought of Justin knowing about his gay BDSM magazines and e-books. "Wait, so you *are* Dominant," he began, and Justin gave him an ironic snort. "Of course you are. But I thought... I mean, you've always had girls...."

"I have dated girls, yes."

"So girls are for dating, but you do, uh, scenes with guys?" he ventured hesitantly.

Justin gave him a reassuring smile as he clarified, "I've dated girls, and I've been with guys casually. I've scened with both."

Chaz suddenly couldn't breathe. *Been with guys...casually?* His heart dropped with a thud as his brain connected the dots.

Justin knew he was gay. Justin had been with other guys — he was gay, or, more appropriately, bi.

And Justin had known that Chaz was gay all this time but had never touched him, never considered him, never wanted him...

His stomach churned and for a long, nerve-racking moment Chaz felt like he might vomit. He felt utterly betrayed. Never mind that they were only roommates and friends. Even though he knew it was unreasonable to be jealous of those faceless *casual* guys, he felt a burning tightness in his chest that rose to his throat, and knew that if he didn't leave in that instant, he might do something completely out of character.

Without a word, he stood and walked across the room to his bed. Past caring about his dignity at this point, he shucked off the stained swim trunks, wincing as the dried cum stuck them to his skin, pulling what felt like a patch of hair off when he heedlessly ripped them down. He didn't bother to clean up, pulling on a pair of jeans and a golf shirt before sliding his feet into his sandals. Next he gathered his watch, wallet, keys and phone, which he flipped open, hitting Andy's number on speed dial.

"Chaz?" Andy answered after just one ring.

"Hi, it's me. Listen, I need a ride."

Justin walked over next to him, but Chaz refused to look up as he walked toward the door.

"Hey there. A ride? Sure, but I thought you were at the beach..." Andy quizzed.

At the same time Justin asked, "Charlie, what's wrong?" and planted himself in front of him, lightly taking hold of his arms.

Chaz did look up then as he reached for the doorknob. Pain shimmered in his eyes as the tears welled up. "Hold on," he told Andy.

"Chaz, don't go." Justin ran his hands up and down his arms soothingly. "Tell me what's bothering you. What we did was—"

"A mistake," Chaz finished with gritted teeth.

Justin froze. "You don't mean that." He pierced him with a searching look, his hands stilled on his arms.

Chaz turned away unimpeded as Justin released his grip. He raised the phone to his ear. "Okay, I'm back. Can you come pick me up?"

"Of course, sweetie. Is that Justin I hear kissing your butt? I take it something went to crap?"

"Yeah. I've gotta get out of here. I never should've come." He looked back at Justin, his gaze landing on those familiar full lips.

We never even kissed.

The thought made him unbearably sad.

"We're on our way. Hope you don't mind Hugh tagging along."

"Thanks a million, Andy. No, I don't mind if Hugh is with

us. The more, the merrier — that's what I hear, anyway," he joked flatly.

He didn't spare another look at the still form of his roommate, who appeared rooted to the floor as Chaz brushed past him out of the door.

I'm not even worth trying to stop.

He walked down the stairs and through the house to the front door, barely drawing a glance from the other guys sitting around the table playing poker. He felt like a ghost, unseen and irrelevant, as he started walking toward the highway, his heart missing from his chest, left on the floor at Justin's feet.

Chapter Seven

Justin stood as though rooted to the floor, frantically trying to rewind the conversation and figure out what had gone so damn wrong. He'd been so convinced, both by Charlie's responsiveness and by his own words about always wanting him, that tonight had been a positive start to a future together.

How had it gone from that to a 'mistake'?

Had he pushed Charlie too far too fast? Should they have waited to talk it through before doing anything sexual? Perhaps, but Justin knew he hadn't imagined Charlie's assent and enjoyment, even of the initial part when he'd impulsively tied Charlie to the bed, tired of him avoiding conversations and pulling his recent disappearing acts.

Charlie had relaxed with total trust. Justin hadn't been imagining that, nor had he been wrong about Charlie's pleasure in his touch. They'd shared an intimate connection as Justin had moved on from ensuring Charlie's pleasure to taking his own, wanting to see Charlie's eyes as he'd removed the blindfold before he came to his peak. There had been a mutual connection there. It was only in the aftermath that Charlie had retreated from him, but even that was understandable. The scene had been intense and a huge alteration to their long relationship. Justin had immediately moved into aftercare mode and tried to soothe Charlie. And it had gone as Justin might have predicted until they'd started talking about Justin's bent.

Had the reality of what Justin enjoyed been too much information right then...?

A knock at the door pulled him from his frantic

examination of the past few minutes.

Charlie…

Hope leaped then quickly crashed as Byron opened the door and poked his head in. He glanced around the room then came the rest of the way inside and closed the door behind him.

"Justin? What happened with Chaz?" His friend took his upper arms in a grip and gave him a sympathetic look. "What's wrong?"

Justin just shook his head. He still had no idea.

Byron gave him a slight shake. "Where is Chaz going? He just walked out the door without a word. Did he…?" Byron paused. "Wasn't he into it? Or…" Byron's eyes went wide. "He isn't a top, is he?"

That penetrated and Justin gave a mirthless laugh. "No, not even close. I… I honestly don't know what happened. We… Everything seemed to go well at first. He told me that he's been avoiding me because he's always been interested in me."

Byron frowned. "That doesn't make sense."

Justin raised his eyebrows. "He thought I was straight."

"Ah." Byron quirked his mouth. "That would do it, I suppose. I always told you to get off the fence."

"Shut up." Justin turned and Byron dropped his hold on him. "You know why I dated women, and I do like them. I just like…" He trailed off.

"You like Chaz more. I know. So…he likes you and you like him. And your kinks align…?" It was more a question than a statement and Justin nodded. Byron continued, "So why did he run?"

"Something afterwards. Something I said…" Justin racked his brain, trying to trace the conversation. "He was asking questions and it seemed to be going okay. I was trying to reassure him about the dating women thing."

He mentally reviewed that part of the conversation — the last thing, now that he thought about it, before Charlie had retreated. "He wanted to know how men and women fit into my life. I understand why, since he only ever saw me with girls. I just couldn't date another man, not with how I feel about him. I explained that while I've dated girls, I've been with guys casually and I've scened with both. I was trying to assure him that the way I feel about him—being with a man—wasn't just a whim..."

"For such a smart guy, you're an idiot," Byron pronounced, wearing a disgusted expression.

"Hey. What the hell?" Justin focused on his friend.

"Dude, you basically just told him that you've fucked around with other guys—both as hook-ups and in scenes. If he likes you, you don't think that probably bothered him?"

Justin's stomach flipped as that sank in. "Fuck."

"Yeah. Don't you think you'd better go after him? I think he has some special attention and reassurance due, and you don't have much time to make this right before your flight."

Justin was already grabbing his keys and his phone off the dresser then whirling toward the door.

"Shirt and shoes," Byron reminded him.

"Oh, right." Justin's gaze flicked to the bed, where the remains of his favorite T-shirt hung in a sad reminder of their brief moment of togetherness. He snatched the first shirt he saw in his suitcase, which he'd never unpacked, then scanned the floor for his flip-flops. "Thanks, By."

"Any time. Now, go get him."

Justin pounded down the stairs and ignored the startled looks from the guys at the table as he jogged past without answering their various queries. Once he'd gotten outside, he looked around the house for a few minutes, just in case Charlie had changed his mind about leaving and was just getting some air. No sign of him.

He pulled out his phone and dialed Charlie's phone, listening for the ring tone, but not hearing anything except what was coming from his own phone. He hung up when it went to voicemail, not leaving a message.

Justin drove slowly along the most direct route the few blocks to the main coastal highway without catching sign of Charlie. There he paused, trying to figure out which way he might have gone. The house was located in a town about halfway between two major highways over the Coast Range. They'd come over the one to the north, but it was about the same distance in the other direction. Who knew which way Andy had told Charlie he would come?

He gritted his teeth at the thought of Andy. Oh, he was a good enough neighbor, Justin supposed, and was a supportive friend to Charlie, but now that Justin had confirmation that Charlie was gay, he just *knew* they'd messed around before. The idea that Andy might take advantage of Charlie's upset and comfort him sent darts of jealousy through Justin. He'd wanted to cement the new side of their relationship before he left town, and he'd be lying if he didn't admit that part of his desire to do so beforehand rather than waiting until he got back was so that Charlie wouldn't turn to Andy while Justin was gone.

Just find him, and you might not have to worry about that.

Mentally crossing his fingers, Justin turned left and began driving as slowly as he dared along the highway, scanning the sides of the road for any sign of a pedestrian who might turn out to be Charlie.

He drove at least three miles, well out of the sprawling coastal town, before he was absolutely certain that Charlie couldn't have gone this way. *Fuck.* He turned around and went back the other way at a more rapid pace, still keeping an eye out in case Charlie had somehow escaped his notice, but wanting to check the other direction before his friend got across the mountains and picked him up. He checked the time and did some mental calculations. No way Andy was anywhere close yet, even if he'd left their apartment complex right away and driven like a maniac.

Justin drove along the highway even farther in that direction, growing more frustrated with every traffic signal and mile marker that passed. Charlie wouldn't have hitchhiked, would he? Panicking, Justin gave in and tried dialing Charlie again, and this time it went directly to voicemail.

"Damn it!" He pounded the steering wheel with the heel of his hand. Blowing out a breath, he tried to think. There were several businesses still open all along the route, including a big chain grocery store, hotels, some fast food and sit down restaurants and bars, and, of course, the casino...

His mind seized upon that possibility. Maybe Charlie had arranged to wait for Andy at the twenty-four-hour casino. That seemed more logical than him either hitchhiking or turning invisible. Some random restaurant or the store might also be options, but it would be a lot less conspicuous to linger for at least an hour in the casino than in the other places, and Justin knew that Charlie didn't like to call undue attention to himself.

Hope growing that he'd finally figured out where Charlie had disappeared to, Justin turned his car around once more and drove back to the area of town nearest the beach house. He still eyed every open business he passed, hoping for a glimpse of Charlie's blond head, but had to reluctantly admit to himself that Charlie could be anywhere. It was the biggest coastal town in this part of the state, and had spread over miles and miles along the coast, actually melding several smaller towns together. This time of night it was easy driving, but during the day, traffic backed up as people made their way through the complex of tourist services.

The casino was a long shot, but the best place he could come up with — it was where he'd wait if he was in the same situation...

That right there brought it home to Justin that it was likely he wouldn't find Charlie there, though he was still going to try. Justin and Charlie couldn't be more different in how they approached situations, so what Justin would do was probably the polar opposite of what Charlie would decide on. And who knew? Maybe Andy had told him where to wait, and it was anyone's guess what that cocky little twink would come up with.

After he'd parked in the casino's lot and gone inside, Justin thoroughly searched the huge floor of the casino and the various eateries inside before conceding defeat. There was no way he was going to find Charlie when he didn't want to be found.

Heart aching, he returned to the beach house and avoided his friends other than giving Byron a quick shake of the head before walking back upstairs.

In the privacy of their room, he sat heavily on the bed and pulled out his phone. It still went to voicemail, but this time he left a brief message. "Charlie... Call me. I'm still at the beach house if you want to come back." He hung up and debated about driving home, but just in case Charlie was cooling off and did end up returning, he'd give it until tomorrow morning.

Charlie's discarded suit was still on the floor, so Justin picked it up. The dangling strips of his T-shirt caught his attention. He tried to remind himself of the positive part of their chemistry and pleasure earlier. They'd been best friends for years and years. Hopefully they'd be able to get through this, but the time ticking away was an added pressure that Justin was having a hard time dealing with. He worked at the knots and removed all the bindings, then picked up the strip he'd used as a blindfold and wrapped it all up with Charlie's suit and tucked them into his suitcase.

Not in the mood to face the guys, he finished packing both his stuff and Charlie's in preparation for leaving in the morning then got ready for bed. But sleep was slow in coming. At some point, though, he drifted off, his silent phone still in his hand.

Chapter Eight

Initially, while Chaz had walked blindly through the quiet streets toward the highway, a part of him had expected Justin to catch up with him at any moment, apologizing, declaring his love, demanding answers, offering a ride, something. *Anything.*

His phone *had* rung at one point with Justin's ring tone as he'd gotten to the coastal highway, and he'd frozen for a moment. He had no idea what to say and had let it ring until it went to voicemail. Then he'd barely breathed while waiting for the message to hit his phone... But it had never come. Justin had evidently chosen not to leave a voicemail.

At that point, he'd called Andy back.

"Hey there, hon. We're driving, but it'll be a while."

Hugh had spoken up in the background, "Tell him to hole up somewhere. I suggest that Denny's near the casino. He shouldn't be walking the highway at night."

"Did you hear that?" Andy asked him. "I completely agree."

"I'm a guy. No one's going to kidnap me or anything," Chaz protested.

"I'm more worried about you getting hit by a drunk or distracted driver who doesn't see you in the dark."

That was actually a good point. "Okay. I'm maybe about... ten blocks from the casino. I didn't eat dinner, so I'll..." He shrugged. He really didn't have an appetite right then, but it would be something to do to pass the time until the guys got over the mountains.

"Okay, honey. We'll see you there in about an hour or so."

"Take your time and be safe," Chaz felt obligated to warn his friend, although he'd bet a million dollars that Hugh — a deputy with the sheriff's department — would have insisted on driving. He was glad that Hugh wasn't working tonight, otherwise he probably would have called Andy back and told him not to make the drive.

"We will. You just get your ass to the Denny's safely. Don't take rides from strangers."

"I won't." He swallowed. "Thanks, Andy."

They said their goodbyes, then Chaz eyed his phone, debating for a moment before turning it off. He didn't think he could let another call from Justin go unanswered, but he couldn't imagine having a conversation with him just then.

He made it to the restaurant and got a booth to himself, turning over the mug for coffee then scanning the extensive menu. Too many choices. He flipped to the breakfast pages and when the waitress came to fill his cup, he went ahead and ordered a strawberry and whipped cream topped Belgian waffle that looked more like dessert than breakfast. He'd probably have a huge sugar rush then crash later on, but it was the only thing that appealed to him.

Andy and Hugh walked in while he was on his third refill of the weak coffee. "Your phone is off," Andy scolded him in greeting even as he pulled Chaz into a tight hug. Hugh gave him a nod then slid into the other side of the booth.

"Aren't we going?" Chaz asked when Andy sat down next to him, trapping him in his seat.

"Need some coffee before we do that drive again," Hugh answered with a slight smile and guilt immediately suffused Chaz.

He flushed and tried to apologize. "Oh God, I'm so sor — "

"Quit it. You needed help and of course I came. And Hugh wasn't about to let me drive to the beach in the dark." Andy slid over to throw an arm around his shoulders. "I won't even ask what he did, but..." He trailed off invitingly.

Chaz shook his head. So much had happened tonight, so many emotional highs and lows, that his brain was a swirling mass of confusion at the moment.

Andy, and to a lesser extent Hugh, tried their best to draw him out over their hastily drunk cups of coffee. Hugh had to work in the morning, so they couldn't linger. That of course made Chaz feel even worse about going off half-cocked and asking for their help.

Ten minutes later they'd left money on the table to cover the bill and had climbed into Hugh's car for the long ride home. Andy, sitting next to him in the back seat, hinted at questions from time to time, and thankfully didn't take it personally when Chaz didn't volunteer much. He'd probably fill Andy in later, but needed to process things first. That, and he didn't want to make Hugh uncomfortable. Even though he and Andy were lovers, he was totally in the closet, and Chaz wasn't sure he wanted to hear about other guys' kinky gay sex.

Of course, Andy, knowing of his one-sided love for Justin, had probably guessed that something intimate had finally happened. But Chaz kept mum and eventually the two gave up, switching to a meaningless and utterly comforting gossip session instead. Chaz leaned back and half listened until they were within a mile of home.

"Oh, shit! I can't stay in the apartment tonight," Chaz exclaimed. "That's the first place he'll...uh..." He trailed off as Andy started nodding with an evil smile.

"Don't worry, sweetie—we already thought of that. We're going to our places, but just to pick up our can't-live-withouts then we're going to have a nice little ménage sleepover at Hugh's until the big brute gets his ass out of town."

Ménage?

"Sleepover? Umm... I..." Chaz stammered, hoping that that didn't mean what he thought it might mean.

Hugh shook his head at Andy in the rear-view mirror. "See? Now he thinks we have ulterior motives."

"Seriously, hon, did you really think we were going to let you ride for free?" Andy batted his eyelashes theatrically at

Chaz, who sagged in relief and glared at his friend as Hugh parked the car in front of their building.

After a silent exchange of glances with Andy, Hugh didn't make a move to get out of the car. Chaz figured that meant Andy was going to try to get him to talk as they went to the outdoors staircase up to their shared top floor landing. But thankfully, Andy remained as quiet as Chaz, at least until they were halfway up.

"Um... Hey."

"What?" Chaz responded, then realized that Andy wasn't talking to him, but to the guy who lived in the apartment under Andy's — Marty...who was currently standing naked in front of his neighbor Kevin's door. Chaz swallowed down an inappropriate giggle at catching him outside in the buff.

Marty and Kevin? He'd thought that they were friends and no more, but evidently they were friends with benefits.

Strange — even though they were only a few yards away and not being quiet, Marty didn't seem to register their presence at all, which didn't fit with what Chaz knew about his rather reserved nature.

"Hi, guys," came a voice from behind them. Kevin, the guy on Marty's floor with the apartment below Chaz and Justin, came trotting up the stairs to where they were frozen in place on the steps in his way. They parted to let him by. "Everything okay? Oh!" Kevin hustled over to place a gentle hand on Marty's back then unlocked his front door. "Kinda early tonight, aren't you, babe? He sleepwalks," Kevin explained in an aside to Chaz and Andy. "Weird, huh?"

"Um, yeah. He might want to think about wearing some clothes to bed," Chaz managed without laughing.

"Oh, let's not be hasty. I'm not minding the view. Always liked natural redheads," Andy joked.

Kevin narrowed his eyes at Andy then ushered Marty into his place. "Move along, nothing to see here."

"Yeah, yeah. I don't blame you for wanting to keep him

to yourself." Andy looked at Chaz as Kevin shut the door. "What? Can you blame me for checking him out?"

"Nope, not really." Chaz chuckled. He couldn't wait to tell Justin about...

Oh. He sobered. For a moment, he'd forgotten about the weirdness between them. He was sure it was only the first of many times he would instinctively revert to their long platonic friendship. But could they go back to that now?

Chaz and Andy went their separate ways at the top of the stairs to gather essentials for the night, and as Chaz let himself into the apartment, he was embraced by evidence of his long friendship with Justin. Their home even smelled like him.

Now that he'd had time to cool down, he knew that he couldn't let their friendship die because he had made the mistake of mixing up sex with love. So what if Justin wasn't interested in him that way? He swallowed, but stiffened his spine. They could still be friends. Maybe even friends with benefits now and then. Now that everything was out on the table, he rationalized, they could go back to how they had been before. Especially since Justin would be gone for the summer, and the memories would have a chance to fade for both of them.

What would he do if Justin only wanted to play with him, keep it casual? He had said he wanted to bring him into the scene after his trip. Chaz warmed at the recollection. Obviously, Justin had gotten a correct read on Chaz and knew about his tendencies in that direction. After Chaz had gotten over his initial shock at being tied up and disciplined into confessing, there was no denying that his years-long love and desire to please Justin had made that step seem like a weird sort of natural progression. But he wasn't sure if he could keep his heart out of anything including Justin, much less something that seemed so...intimate.

He got ready to leave then paused. He didn't want to talk to Justin yet, but he didn't want him to worry, either. He made a quick decision, and after deliberating on the wording for some time, scrawled out a note.

Staying with friends. Have a great trip. See you when you get back. Safe travels, Charlie

After dropping the note onto Justin's bed, he quickly locked up and met Andy and Hugh down at the car.

"Ready?" Andy asked, his usually animated face sober and sympathetic.

Chaz gave him a ghost of a smile and nodded, hoping like hell that he was doing the right thing.

Chapter Nine

Justin was exhausted by the time he exited the highway on the way home the next morning. He'd tried calling Charlie once more before he'd left the coast, but it had again gone straight to voicemail. Not bothering to leave a message, he'd prepared to leave.

Both Cody and Byron had offered to ride back with him, but he hadn't been in the mood for company. He was frustrated by Charlie's refusal to talk to him, and disappointed in himself for not handling the situation better. He tried to keep from overanalyzing it during the drive and completed the drive home by rote, sagging in relief when he saw that both Charlie's and Andy's cars were parked in their usual spots.

He left his things in the car and took the stairs to their landing two at a time. After drawing a couple of deep breaths to try to settle himself, he unlocked the door and went inside.

Almost immediately, he could tell that Charlie wasn't there. The apartment had a still, undisturbed quality to it. "Fuck." He pulled out his phone as he walked back to confirm that, no, Charlie wasn't in his bedroom. His bed was made and nothing appeared out of place…

Voicemail again. "Charlie, it's me. I'm back home, and you're not here. I'm really worried about you — please call." God, what if Andy hadn't found him either?

He hung up and strode to the front door, then across the landing to pound on Andy's door until his hand hurt. No answer, and no sounds from inside either. Why the hell hadn't he ever gotten Andy's number?

Justin scrolled through the history on his phone, just on the off chance that Charlie might have called him from Andy's at some point.

Damn it, this is futile.

It was only around twenty-four hours until his flight. He didn't have time for this. The time moving ever onward was pressing on him like being deep underwater.

Stymied at every turn, he finally started to lose his usually endless patience. He jabbed at the phone to call again and gritted his teeth at the same voicemail message he was getting heartily sick of hearing. At the tone he said, "Okay, it's me again. Nobody's answering the door at your twink friend's apartment. Where the hell are you?" He hung up before he could say more then walked into the apartment, already redialing. "Charlie, call me right the fuck now!"

Fuck, now he was yelling like an idiot. A jealous idiot.

He ran a hand through his hair and shoved the phone into his pocket, vowing not to call him again until he'd gotten his emotions under control. To that end he walked back down to his car, gathered his bag and computer case, then locked up and carried it all back up to the apartment.

He kicked the front door shut behind him and went through to his bedroom. When he tossed the bag onto the bed in the dimness, he heard a crinkle.

After hastily fumbling to turn on the bedside light, he finally was able to see what he'd missed before—a short note written in Charlie's distinctive scrawl. "Friends," Justin echoed. Other than the guys back at the beach house, Charlie only counted a couple of other people as his friends—Justin and Andy. So Charlie's note must mean Andy and his current guy, the straight-passing cop boyfriend.

That brought up another level of worry. Plus he owed Charlie an apology for his last message since he *had* left him a note. God, it was going to be embarrassing how many stupid voicemails Charlie was going to get if he ever turned his freaking phone back on.

He pulled his out and hit redial. "Hi, sorry. I found your note. I'm guessing you're with Andy at his boyfriend's, but" — how to say it without sounding like a jerk? — "just don't do anything stupid, okay?" Yeah, that wasn't going to work but he couldn't take the words back. He hung up before he could make even more of an ass out of himself.

Pacing back and forth a few times, he rolled his eyes at himself. Fuck it. He dialed again. Ring, leave a message... Lather, rinse, repeat. God, he was losing his mind. "Hey. Me again. I didn't mean to say stupid. I just meant, don't do anything you can't take back. Please. I'll be here packing all day today, so call me back." He sighed then disconnected.

Justin looked at the stacks of stuff all over the room. He really needed to get to work.

First, laundry. Hopefully Charlie would be home soon, and maybe he could salvage a little bit of what he'd wanted to accomplish between them before he left on his volunteer trip.

Please come home, Charlie. Call me, or come home.

* * * *

Chaz kept his cell phone turned off while he stayed with Andy at Hugh's, and deliberately waited until he knew that Justin's flight had gone before having Hugh take him and Andy home. Andy had accompanied him into the apartment for support, and it was obvious right away that Justin had gone.

He could see the bag he'd taken to the beach sitting in the hallway by his bedroom door, and he wondered if Justin had put the cummy swimsuit in there or just thrown it away.

"He's gone." Rather than just a statement, it came out a bit unsteady, and Andy squeezed Chaz's arm as he cleared his throat and continued, "That's that, then."

"It'll work out, hon."

Chaz shot his well-meaning friend a skeptical glance.

Right now it didn't feel like anything was going to go right ever again.

"Fine. That was a useless platitude," Andy admitted, "but honestly, I think a bit of time apart isn't going to hurt, and it just might help you get a handle on it all. And it sounds like it was a hell of a goodbye, probably more than would have happened if you hadn't played hard to get."

His jaw dropped. "I didn't play hard to get!"

"Not on purpose maybe, but if it looks like a duck and quacks like a duck..." Andy leered at him, arching his eyebrow. "Hey, it got the job done. At least one of you finally made a move, however it started."

Chaz didn't want to admit it to him, but Andy was a pretty smart guy. And under the snarky attitude he affected, he was a caring person.

"So, are you going to just play with it all night?"

"What?" Chaz had no idea how to interpret that question out of left field. "Just... What?"

Andy rolled his eyes dramatically then gestured to his hand. "Your phone. You've been toying with it for a half hour. You can press the power button any time now."

He'd had no idea he was even holding it. Not surprising that he'd block it out. He suspected that he'd probably gotten at least one message from Justin, and was dreading hearing what he had to say. At the same time, he really wanted to hear his voice, hear the goodbye he'd denied them.

Bracing himself, he turned on the phone and waited impatiently as it booted up. He winced when the notifications popped up that he did indeed have voicemail. After he dialed in, he put it on speaker so that Andy could hear too. That way he wouldn't have to repeat whatever he said.

They started to play and became increasingly hard to listen to. Justin had left a simple, predictable one that first night, then several yesterday, varying in tone from pleading to frustrated and back again. Chaz swallowed hard when

Justin had begged him not to do anything with Andy and Hugh. As if he would, but the fact that Justin cared gave him a warm feeling.

Then he hit the ones from today.

"*Hi, good morning.*" A long deep breath and a sigh. "*I have to leave for the airport any minute, but I can wait outside security in the international terminal for a little while, if you maybe want to come see me off. Okay, bye.*"

"Oh God." Chaz pictured Justin pacing by the security line, looking over the crowd for him before finally giving up and getting in line. It was a sickeningly clear image that made his heart hurt. He should have been there, should have been the one to take him instead of him taking a cab or something, even just as his friend.

"*Hey, it's me. I'm at the airport.*" Another long pause. "*I guess I had this fantasy that you'd be here to hug me goodbye. I can't believe that I'm going without seeing you. I almost didn't leave, but I made this commitment, and, well, we were solid back then, so I thought, what's two months?*" A sad little laugh. "*Anyway, they're boarding. I'll call you soon as I can. Bye, guy.*"

That last was in a low, intimate tone of voice.

"*Hi, Charlie. I'm on the plane and I'll have to turn my phone off in a minute. I wish you were here with me. Anyway, I left you a note today, plus there's a package in your bedside table drawer that I'd put in there right before the beach house trip. I forgot to take it out with everything going on. I understand if what's in there is out of the question and hope it doesn't make you mad. I...planned it before all this. Anyway, I need you to know that, if you want to still go back to the way we were, I really want that too. I miss you. I'll take you any way I can get you, Charlie. Best friends, right? Bye.*"

Chaz sat heavily on the couch and looked at Andy. One tear escaped and trickled down his cheek. "I should've seen him before he left. Damn it, I'm so stupid. Why didn't I take his calls? I should have come home instead of trying to prove something. What was I thinking?"

Andy smiled sympathetically even as he smacked him

lightly on the back of the head. "That both of you needed space to get your heads in the right place. If you'd stayed, or been here, or answered, it might not've been enough time yet. That's when people say things they regret or do things they wouldn't normally. *Capice?*"

Chaz groaned while he rubbed his head then frowned. "He said he left me something before all this happened? What does that mean?"

Andy shrugged. "Go into your room and take a look. You'll figure it out. If it's in your bedside table, it's probably not for my viewing pleasure." He patted Chaz's shoulder and walked toward the front door. "Let me know if I can help you with anything." He tilted his head then winked. "Well, maybe not *anything*. But you know what I mean. Seriously, call me if you need me. I'll check back in later." Andy's smile was genuine and supportive as he carefully closed the door behind him.

Alone in the apartment, Chaz made himself walk at a normal speed toward his bedroom, when he really wanted to race in and find whatever Justin had left, needing that connection to him. Once inside, he went immediately to his bedside table, pulling the top drawer open. Nothing. Frowning, he checked the second drawer and froze when he saw a large, padded envelope with his name on it. He picked it up—it was surprisingly heavy and bulky—and ripped it open. He gaped in amazement as a folded note and several smaller envelopes fell out and landed on the mattress. He chose a smallish one at random and opened it then flushed, even without an audience.

Oh, come on. People use these things every day. Nobody's here. You can at least look at them.

He was very glad that Andy had been intuitive enough not to be here for the opening. It was an interesting metal object made up of three rings. He turned it this way and that. Cock ring. He'd never seen one in person, and there was no way he was asking Andy for help. He'd wait to see what he could find out about it online. Rather than open another one, he picked up the note and unfolded it to read.

Hi, Charlie… Been trying to decide whether to be on the phone with you when you open this or not. I think I'll tell you about it and have you call me back so you can blush alone.

Jeez, apparently Justin and Andy had been trading notes on him or something.

Apparently our conversation about this went well enough for me to leave this here for you. Two months is a long time to be missing you, but it will give you a chance to have some fun, expand your horizons and get ready for when I get back in August. The more you wear the plugs, the more accustomed you'll get to being stretched. Much better for both of us. Use plenty of lube, and don't go up in size too quickly – you have plenty of time.

The ring is for training you to hold off orgasm. Slip into it before you get fully hard, balls first, then your pretty cock. I have a nice leather one I'll give you when I get back.

You have your instructions about jerking off. Be sure to follow them – I will be checking in.

I love you, J

Chaz sat silent on his bed, staring at the note, in complete and utter shock and lust at its contents. Snippets jumped off the page at him.

…ready for when I get back… Much better for both of us… your pretty cock… I love you, J.

I love you…

Wait, there was supposed to be another note written today somewhere from what he'd said in his voicemail. He looked around frantically before practically running down the hall, backing up just as fast as he passed Justin's room. There – on the bed, just where he had left his own note. He snatched it up and read.

Charlie, I never dreamed I would have to put this all in a note instead of watching your face while I said it. But I can't go off for the summer without letting you know how I feel. You're my best friend, and I can't imagine my life without you. I don't want to lose you. I'm not positive why you got so upset at the cottage, but after thinking about it, I realized it happened after I talked about being with other men. I've hoped for a while now that you might feel more for me than just friendship, but when you weren't comfortable telling me you were gay, I thought you weren't interested in me. But after remembering the beautiful way you came for me at the beach, I started thinking (hoping?) that maybe you were upset because you were jealous.

Let me tell you exactly why I used the word 'casual' for those men – because I love you. And even when I didn't think I could have you, I felt like anything with anyone else was cheating. Yes, I've done a few things at the clubs, but you would be surprised at how seldom that was and how little was done.

I want you to think about us for the next couple months, about whether you can see giving us a try as a couple, or if we can still be best friends. Those are the only two options I'm leaving you, and I strongly suggest both. Take care – be safe – love you, J

The next two months loomed in front of Chaz endlessly.

Chapter Ten

When Justin had first arrived La Aurora airport in Guatemala, he had been almost ill from having to leave without hearing from Charlie. Despite the encouraging words he'd left for Charlie in the letter on his bed, he feared that the misunderstanding between them would fester rather than fade. He'd gone two days without seeing Charlie—well, nearly three by the time he'd arrived at the organization's office in Antigua—and he ached with missing Charlie already. Two months was going to seem like forever.

Once he was out in the settlement where he'd be working for the majority of the time he was here, he wouldn't have access to either phone or Internet, so if he was going to contact Charlie, it would have to be before he left the city. Whether or not it would be too soon, he couldn't help that. He'd have to hope for the best.

First, though, he had to fight through his travel weariness and jump into the demanding orientation to his volunteer program with the rest of his team. That meant long days when he didn't have a spare minute to think, and all he wanted to do at the end of the day was sleep. Finally, they got the news that they had one free day before they'd depart, to use to rest, shop for supplies or spend extra time working on skill building.

One of the organization's team leaders had given him a basic cell phone from Mexico and he'd had the SIM card switched to a local one easily enough. The rate to call back to the US wasn't terrible, but with the cost of the rates in the other direction, he'd need to warn everyone not to call him unless it was an emergency, and even then, just leave their name and hang up then he'd call them back when he could. Email was another option, though again, same as with phone coverage, access to a computer would only be possible when he was in the city, and he'd just as soon keep it short but be able to hear people's voices.

To hear Charlie's voice.

The two other newly arrived volunteers he was sharing a room with, Carlos and Luke, had both gone out to do some shopping, leaving him with combined free time and privacy for the first time in the week he'd been there.

Taking a deep breath for courage, he typed in Charlie's phone number then hit call.

Three rings later he was so tightly strung that he had to remind himself to breathe. He sat down on his bunk. Was Charlie still avoiding his calls? Or maybe he just wasn't answering because he didn't recognize the number...

"Hello?"

There was a slight echo but it was definitely Charlie's voice. Relief made him dizzy. "Charlie? It's me."

He heard an indrawn breath. "Justin? Oh my God. I had no idea I'd hear from you."

"It won't happen too often—not much phone coverage where I'll be heading tomorrow, which is why I'm calling today. Finally got a day off and"—he shrugged then lay back, pillowing his head on his free arm—"I wanted to hear your voice. I miss you," he admitted.

"Oh. I miss you too. This week has sucked...and not in the good way."

Justin chuckled, glad that they were back to joking around. Maybe this separation wouldn't be a disaster after all. "Look, I really want to—"

"No!" Charlie interrupted. "If you're trying to apologize or something, stop it. *I'm* the one who freaked out. I'm embarrassed as hell that I went storming off into the night just because you...aren't a virgin."

The last thing Justin wanted was to go there again, but he

had to make it clear about the people in his past. "I could have handled it better. Not exactly great afterglow to bring it up right then. I had some idea that it would set your mind at ease, that I wasn't just...gay for you on a whim..." God, he needed to zip his lips. "Okay, I'm doing it again. Shutting up now."

Charlie snorted. "There's nothing wrong with being gay for you...uh, me. It's not like there's a prize for being the *most* gay. Or one hundred percent gay. I get that you can...appreciate both sexes. I..." He paused then cleared his throat. "I guess I just worry that if we were to...you know...get together that way, you might eventually miss women." By the end, his voice was nearly a whisper.

Justin sat up, shaking his head, even though he knew that Charlie couldn't see him. "No way. I won't have any trouble staying with one sex for the rest of my life."

"You've only ever dated women." Charlie's voice was suddenly rough and so serious. "How can you say that?"

The truth came spilling out, necessary in that moment. This short conversation had become so intense. "I couldn't date other men because they weren't you. There's only one man I've ever wanted" —*loved*— "and if I couldn't have you, I didn't want any man in my life. Charlie, if we can do this, make this transition, I'll have everything I would ever want. I want to be that for you, too." He knew that this would be the last call they would have to talk together for an unknown amount of time, and felt the urgent need to come to some sense of stability. An agreement to see it through.

Charlie blew out a breath. "I feel like there's so much to talk about, but I have no idea how long you have."

"Not long enough, probably, so why don't you tell me what you need to hear the most?"

The silence rang between them for several precious moments. "Um..."

"Did you open the envelope?" he asked in an attempt to break the ice and talk about the elephant in the room.

"And read the letter?" He was also interested in Charlie's reaction, and he had a feeling he wouldn't be disappointed.

"Yes. Well... Um, not all of it. Oh, man..."

"What did you find so far?" he coaxed, enjoying the huskiness that betrayed Charlie's arousal.

"The, uh...cock ring."

It was crazy how close they were, and yet there were so many things unknown. "You know," he started in a conversational voice, "I've touched your dick, but I've never seen it—at least not fully erect. I've gotten looks at other times over the years, though."

Charlie exhaled hard and the sound went straight to Justin's cock, which was now semi-erect. He lay back down and cupped it, wishing he had a private room with a lock.

"But you saw mine that night. Do you remember?"

"Yes." It was almost a hiss, and Justin wondered if Charlie was touching himself as well.

"I was just trying to picture your cock and balls in the cock ring. Have you tried it on?"

"Justin..."

"What?"

Charlie groaned. "This is hard."

Justin pretended to misunderstand. "I'm hard too."

A gasp from the other end of the line. "Oh. I didn't mean... I meant, it's hard talking about it."

"It's a yes–no question, Charlie. So... Yes or no?"

"Yes."

Satisfied by his admission, Justin changed gears and asked, "Is there anything in either of my letters you want to talk about while we're able to talk?" He wondered if Charlie had picked up the part about rules for bringing himself off.

"The part where you said...about jerking off..."

"You want to know my instructions?" It was a rhetorical question and he continued without waiting for an answer, not that Charlie seemed forthcoming at this point. "Very simple. You need to always use at least one thing that was in the envelope, or you'll have to refrain."

"Is everything in there like…? I mean, what else…?"

"You've only opened the cock ring?"

"Yeah."

That surprised Justin. Charlie had always been so curious. "Well, I'd like you to open one more tonight, but choose wisely. I want you to try out whatever it is you pick. I suggest feeling them through the packaging for comparison." He had to make sure to keep his smile out of his voice, trying to imagine the look on Charlie's face if he were to pick the largest of the plugs first. "And remember, you have to use everything at least once before I come home. Okay?"

"O-okay. But there's one more thing from the letter. Justin…"

"What is it?"

"You really think you love me?"

It was an unexpected question considering their current line of conversation, but on second thought, it all fit together. He supposed that was the true elephant in the room, actually. "I know I do," he answered, confident in how he felt about his best friend, even if he wasn't sure about how they would get through the huge change in their dynamic and the current separation.

"It's weird not seeing you for this long. I know part of it is my fault, but anyway, I don't think we've gone more than maybe a week without seeing each other since we were teenagers. I just…wish you were here."

It truly was weird. "Me too. But we're already a week closer. Look"—he glanced at the time—"I have to go, but I'll call you in two or three weeks when I get back to the city."

"Two or three…?" Charlie sighed. "I shouldn't be disappointed by that. I wasn't sure I'd hear from you at all."

"First chance I get. And you now have this number, but don't call unless it's an emergency. A call this length would cost you the same as a month's rent." He was only exaggerating slightly. "If you do, just leave a message that it's you, and I'll call you back as soon as I get it and have good enough reception to make a call."

"Okay. Sorry this was so expensive."

"Nah—it's not as bad from here, and anyway, it was worth every penny to hear your voice and know that..." Now it was Justin who was unable to finish a sentence.

"I love you," Charlie filled in the blank for them both, and the last bits of apprehension were washed away. "I'm really, really glad you called."

"I'm glad you answered," Justin teased, both to lighten the mood and because it was too good an opening to let pass.

"Ugh." Charlie sounded disgusted. "You just had to bring that up."

"I don't know why you're so bothered by it. *I'm* the crazy-pants who left, like, a hundred messages. 'Call me! Call me right now!'"

They were able to end with a laugh on that note and when Justin disconnected, he was able to breathe for the first time in over a week. He also knew that he'd be discreetly taking care of his erection later on, and that hadn't happened in the same amount of time. His sense of relief was immense, as though a huge weight had been lifted from his chest. The two months ahead didn't seem quite as daunting anymore, knowing that Charlie would be waiting for him when the time was done.

Chapter Eleven

In Justin's bedroom, Chaz dropped his phone to the bed beside him and looked down at the cock ring framing his sac and the base of his semi-hard shaft. He'd been experimenting when the phone rang, and almost hadn't answered, but the unfamiliar number had caught his attention and he was so glad it had. He just wished he'd had the guts to tell Justin he had it on.

He lay back and let out a huge breath. It was almost as though Justin had known he was in his room, or could sense that he was playing with one of the toys he had left. Speaking of which...

Chaz slowly eased his way out of the welded cock ring, barely able to get his partially stiff shaft bent enough to remove it. With a wince, he finally succeeded. He stood, smoothed out Justin's bedspread then went back to his room.

He wasn't sure why he hadn't looked into the rest of Justin's package, but there was no question that he'd do so now that he'd been told to. One today. He'd think about doing the rest at some point.

Very intrigued and a bit nervous about Justin's suggestion that he sort them by feel, he dumped the contents of the large envelope onto his bed and looked the smaller padded packages over. One obviously contained a box. He set that one aside. The three shorter ones looked similar but when he picked them up and used his touch to explore through the packaging, he came to realize that there was a size difference. Those he laid out in order from thinnest to thickest.

The longest one was the one that really snagged his attention. Biting his lip, he held it for a moment. No question that this one was some sort of dildo. He reluctantly placed it next to the boxy one.

The last two packages were sort of round — one was bulky and one almost completely flat, like there was nothing in it. He had no idea at all what could be in those. The flat one might be the safest choice...

But he didn't want to make a choice just to be safe — at least most of him didn't. He firmly set aside that one then went a step further and put it into the big envelope, which was starting to show wear from how often he'd handled it this week.

Justin didn't want him to make the safe choice either, judging from the instructions he'd given to feel them before deciding. Maybe one of the set of three...whatever they were. His fingers danced over the three, even though now he could visually tell what size each was.

Playing it conservative, he put all but the smallest feeling of the three similar objects back into the main package then tucked it into his drawer, which had now become his 'toy drawer'. He'd moved everything else out of it — except for his magazines, of course — found other places to put them, and even relocated his lonely tube of lube from its hiding place in the back of his top drawer.

Other than moving it, he hadn't touched it — or himself — since Justin had left.

Well... He *had* helped his morning erection along, but something about the memory of Justin stating that he would need permission to come from then on had stayed with him.

Intellectually, he knew that Justin probably hadn't meant all the time, and certainly he wouldn't be expected to refrain the entire time Justin was out of town, but the idea held an appeal that had left Chaz most of the way to no return several times before he'd stop and will his erection away.

Glancing down at his burgeoning hard-on, he rolled his

eyes at himself. He hadn't even opened the thing yet. Might as well go ahead at this point. He ripped the top of the envelope open and tipped its contents onto the bed.

His lips parted and he hardened further.

The impact of the plug was given even more impetus by its color—completely black rubber. It was fairly small, with its thin neck above a wider base. He picked it up and the rubber almost immediately warmed in his hand.

'I want you to try out whatever it is you pick...'

Feeling a bit silly, he nevertheless glanced over his shoulder at the open bedroom door. Andy had a key but he'd only ever used it once when Chaz had called him frantically from school one day and had him grab a flashdrive he'd forgotten.

Obviously Justin wasn't going to come walking in—and he'd probably be happy to join in if he ever caught Chaz playing with sex toys. He was getting used to being naked at home since he was drawn to Justin's room, and walked back and forth between their rooms.

This, though, he'd do in here.

He stripped his bedcovers back, tossed the plug next to his pillow then grabbed his lube from the drawer. After lying back, he drew his knees up and flicked the top of the lube open. Although not a complete stranger to self-penetration with a finger or two, Chaz had never had anything else inside him.

Starting with what he knew, he ran some lube along his opening and began to loosen himself up enough to easily take two of his fingers. It was too much when he imagined Justin watching him do this—or doing it himself—so he tried to blank his mind. He wasn't entirely successful, though, and the stimulation kept him at least half hard the whole time.

After adding more lube to his ass than he probably needed, he oiled up the rubber plug. He placed it at his entrance, blew out a breath and began to slowly insert it. It was rather easier going in than he'd thought, and very different from fingers. The heavy material was foreign but its presence stretched his hole without mercy or any give. He was glad that he'd started small, but so far it wasn't a bad experience at all.

Finally, it was all the way in and his hole closed down around the indentation just above the base. Full. Not as full as he'd be with one of the larger options inside him, but… Wow.

No — don't think of Justin. No, no… Oh crap.

He'd been able to keep his cock under control for the most part during the process, up until Justin came to mind. Trying to distract himself, and also curious about how it would feel if he moved around, Chaz swung his legs to the side and sat up.

Oh God.

Now that was…um…interesting.

Whoa.

He gingerly stood. The rubber plug shifted inside him, sending a zing through his balls, and he gasped and froze. Was that his prostate? He'd never been able to find it on his own — either he wasn't flexible enough or his fingers weren't long enough.

Some of the guys in stories he'd read walked around with these inside them on the orders of their Dom, doing normal, everyday things. He tried walking across the room, glad that no one was there to see him as he moaned out loud more than once before he got to the hallway. Bracing himself on the doorjamb, he took a deep breath.

This was going to take some getting used to.

Good thing he had nothing but time.

Chapter Twelve

"Hey, stranger. Want to come over for dinner?"

Chaz winced and put his laptop into hibernation mode while holding the phone against his ear with his shoulder. "Um..."

Andy sighed loudly, sounding irritated. "Hon, Justin's been gone for weeks, and I've barely seen you since he left. It's getting ridiculous. Come over right now or I'm coming to get you," he demanded, and Chaz knew better than to doubt that he would.

"Is that okay with Hugh?" he checked, already walking toward his bedroom.

"First of all, he's not here. He's working second shift this week and that's almost impossible for us to work our schedules around. And it wouldn't matter if he was here. He'd just have to deal."

"Good point." Chaz knew that Andy wasn't one to let anyone run his life...which made it interesting that he continued to stay with a closeted man who wouldn't acknowledge him in public. He opened his own closet and stared inside.

"It's Saturday night. Neither one of us has anything going on tomorrow, so we can work our way through a couple of bottles of wine and not worry about the consequences. Don't worry about what you're wearing, either. It's just me and we're not going anywhere."

Chaz looked down at his T-shirt and jeans dubiously then shrugged. "All right. What can I bring?"

"Just yourself. I have everything we need. You can host next time."

He laughed at that. "Well, when it's my turn you'd better give me some notice. Without Justin here, my cupboards are pretty bare. I keep forgetting to go to the store." After grabbing his keys he let himself out of his apartment and locked it behind him.

"That doesn't surprise me, and it's exactly why I said not to bother with anything. Oh, there you are."

Chaz could hear Andy both in his ear and through his front door. Grinning, he disconnected just as Andy opened to him. "Were you watching for me through the peephole?"

"Well, yeah." He led the way inside and left Chaz to close up behind himself. The apartment was redolent of garlic and onions and maybe some kind of fish?

"Smells great in here," he called to Andy, who had disappeared into the kitchen. He made to follow him and jumped back in a hurry when Andy came around the corner and they almost collided.

"Whoa. Here." Andy handed him a glass of red wine then held his up. "Cheers."

They clinked glasses then Chaz took a sip as Andy retreated into the kitchen once again. Might be a night to regret—the wine tasted dangerously good and he hadn't had anything to eat since a small breakfast. He'd sort of got lost on the Internet. It had started innocently enough with him reading some research in his field of study, then he'd moved on to various news outlets and from there had followed link after link until Andy had called while he was taking a quiz about how many Eighties films he'd seen.

Ugh.

It was probably a good thing he was getting out.

He knew very well that he was hibernating and distracting himself with mindless stuff to keep his thoughts from how much he missed Justin. Summer was his least busy time of year. His class load was halved, and since the campus wasn't as busy, his work study hours in the computer lab were also reduced to two shifts a week. That left him with a lot of free time.

In past summers, he'd spent that excess time doing... well, whatever Justin was in the mood to do. His best friend always came up with great ideas, whether it was jaunting off to a nearby city for a festival, exploring some small, esoteric museum no one had ever heard of, volunteering to pull ivy or paddle down the river and scoop trash from the water, or just heading over to spend time at the beach...

Chaz sighed then took a long drink of wine.

"Don't guzzle it!" Andy came back in, bearing a plate of cheeses, bread and roasted garlic. "Snack time. I don't want you passing out at six o'clock from too much wine on an empty stomach. I just want you happily drunk and at my mercy."

"At your...?" Chaz sputtered. "Hey. I'm not... I don't want to... No offense."

"Relax." Andy stepped over his legs and plopped down next to him on the couch. "I might have nefarious intentions, but they have nothing to do with taking advantage of your body." He gestured with his wine glass. "I know you're mentally wed to Justin. And then I've got Hugh...sort of." Andy scowled into his glass as he took a sip.

"Uh-oh. What's going on with Hugh?" He had been a horrible friend lately. He really needed to pull his head out of his own funk and take an interest in what was happening around him.

"Same old, same old... Which is starting to get old."

Chaz narrowed his gaze at Andy. "No. You don't get all frowny over the same old thing. Something specific happened. What is it?" He nudged Andy's leg with his knee. "Come on. You know you want to tell me. That's probably why you called me to come over for dinner in the first place."

Andy shoved him back with his own knee, being not nearly as gentle.

Chaz lifted his glass trying to keep it from spilling. "Hey! A wine stain on your couch isn't going to help anything."

"Crap. Sorry. You're right." When Andy looked up to

meet Chaz's eyes, Chaz was surprised at the pain he saw reflected there. "Hugh's receiving a commendation from the department tonight at a banquet. Certificate of Merit, I guess it's called. It's kind of a big deal. The deputies don't get awards that often."

"Oh." Chaz leaned over and took Andy into his arms for a long hug. "I'm sorry you can't be there with him. I'm sure he'll miss having someone there for him, too." He sat back but kept his arm around Andy's shoulders.

"That's just it. Another deputy knew he 'didn't have a date'" — Andy snuggled against him and made air quotes — "and set him up. They're going as a foursome with his fiancée and her friend."

Chaz gave him a wordless side hug, because what could he say to that?

"I know he's not interested in her, and he's not the one who went looking for a date, but..." Andy fiddled with the stem of his wine glass. "It just sucks."

"Yeah. Well" — he clinked with Andy — "here's to Hugh the Hero and his award."

"Here, here."

They drained their glasses and Chaz separated himself to stand. "Should I grab the bottle?"

"Better bring the second one too...and the corkscrew."

* * * *

Two hours later they'd polished off two bottles of wine, all of the appetizers, and were eating the paella with two forks out of the pan Andy had set down right onto the coffee table in front of them.

"This is so good." Chaz waved his fork around as he praised his friend, who gave him a huge grin.

"Thanks, honey. You know me and rice."

Chaz gave a high-pitched laugh. He would *not* call it a giggle. "How many people keep six kinds of rice in their pantry? That's just weird."

"At least I have food in my pantry. You know, there's this wonderful place called a grocery store. I should take you sometime. Oh!" He shoveled two bites of paella into his mouth then bounced to his feet. "We should go now! We need more to drink anyway."

Chaz shook his head and grabbed Andy's arm, trying in vain to tug him back down. For a small guy he wasn't very easy to move around. "I'm not driving at this point and neither are you. I'm sure I have wine or beer at my place. Just" — he burst out laughing — "no food."

Andy stared at him a minute then started giggling.

Now *that* was a giggle.

After grabbing the pan of paella, Andy followed Chaz, who had both almost empty wine glasses in his hands, across the landing to his door. Unlocking the door proved challenging, but they managed to get inside without dropping or spilling anything.

Thankfully it wasn't too much of a mess. Even when he was doing his best impression of a shut-in, Chaz was still fairly anal about keeping the apartment clean. Plus it wasn't like there were dirty dishes lying around.

"Well, well... What's this?"

Chaz froze on his way into the kitchen to check for something to drink. Oh God, he hadn't left anything embarrassing out, had he? Panicking, he put down the glasses and ran back into the living room, where Andy had his back to him, studying something in his hands. He'd put the paella on the table, and Chaz struggled to remember whether he'd played with anything out here that Andy might have seen sitting there or on the couch.

Andy turned around and held up a box. "Since when did you get the *Killers* boxed set?"

Chaz sagged with relief, and even with a bottle of wine coursing through his system, Andy didn't miss his reaction.

He cocked his head at Chaz. "What did you *think* I'd found that had you tearing in here like a maniac?"

Opening and closing his mouth a couple of times without

75

managing to get any words out, Chaz finally shook his head. No way Andy wouldn't succeed in getting it out of him.

But first, he needed more wine for this.

"Just" – he gestured vaguely – "hold on a sec. Wine first. If I don't have any, is a beer okay?"

Andy gave him a triumphant smirk, obviously sensing his capitulation. "Whatever, hon. I'm easy." He winked.

"That's what *he* said," Chaz called back over his shoulder. He checked the pantry – no wine. In the fridge there was a bottle of white wine about two-thirds empty. Justin sometimes used a splash of wine while cooking, but he always said that the best wine for that wasn't necessarily good for drinking.

He uncapped two bottles of wheat beer and carried them back in. Andy accepted his, still smiling. It was good to see, actually. If Chaz could keep Andy's mind off his boyfriend's 'date' tonight – and the larger picture of it not looking like Hugh would ever acknowledge him as his – then he'd sacrifice his dignity and privacy.

That's what friends were for.

Chapter Thirteen

"Why won't you let me see them?" Andy whined after Chaz had finished his 'confession' about what he'd been doing since Justin had left. "I've seen you naked. I've even sucked your—"

"Quit it. You really want to see something I've had in my...? Actually, never mind. Don't answer that."

"Still..."

"I know, I know. It's just weird."

Andy sat up and snapped his fingers then pointed at Chaz.

"What?" he asked Andy warily.

"You said you haven't opened some of them. Bring out one and open it now. If you haven't used it, it's not weird. *Voilà.*"

Huh? Chaz shook his head slightly in disbelief. "How do you figure that?"

Andy shrugged and flipped his hand. "It's just like browsing at a store, shopping together." He finished off his beer.

"I've never been shopping at a sex toy store with you!"

"So? C'mon." Andy made beckoning motions with his hand. "Pick one out and let's see it. It'll be just like Christmas."

Chaz just stared at him.

"Oh, come *on*. Humor me. It's not like I'm going to make you *use* it in front of me."

He actually had been worried about just that. Relaxing a bit, Chaz considered it for a minute. He'd decided to open one per week to spread them out, and would be opening one this weekend anyway. Probably wouldn't hurt to indulge Andy's curiosity, especially since he'd backed off from insisting on seeing the whole lot.

Although, that was just Andy's style — ask for the whole enchilada first, which would then make giving him the majority seem reasonable when he 'gave in'.

It was probably a character defect that he was being swayed into going with the flow. Justin was effortless at getting Chaz to do what he wanted, and so was Andy — in different ways, true — but Chaz knew that he could fully trust both of them, so he supposed it wasn't the worst thing in the world. And he knew that if he felt strongly against something, he'd put his foot down. Hopefully.

Andy actually clapped when Chaz stood then walked toward the bedrooms.

"Yeah, yeah. I swear, you always get your way," he complained, and Andy's pleased laughter followed him into his bedroom.

It occurred to him as he sat on his bed that he would have definitely told Andy no if he'd wanted to come in here with him to see it. There was something personal about this space where he'd perched so many times, looking at the contents of Justin's package and selecting the next item.

Since the first slender plug, he'd opened the other two similar envelopes, revealing that it had indeed been a set of three. The other two had been definite challenges, but were becoming easier to use. He'd enjoyed the long one, but the slightly shorter and fattest one was his favorite so far. He couldn't wear it outside the house like he could the first one he'd tried, but he loved the way it stretched him to the limit…like Justin's cock would.

His own dick began to react predictably. Conscious of Andy in the other room, he quickly pulled his thoughts back from that tangent and took out the remaining wrapped items — at this point, he'd dubbed them 'the dildo one', 'the boxy one', 'the bulky one' and 'the flat one'.

Staring at them as though he could see through the

wrapping, he tried to predict which one would be the least embarrassing to open in front of his friend. Problem was, the latter three could be anything, and he had no idea how he'd react to whatever could be in them. Honestly, the dildo one would probably be the best option because at least he wouldn't be surprised while he had an audience.

He tucked the rest back away then he took a deep breath and walked back out into the living room. Andy had been busy for however long he'd been gone. He'd cleaned up all of the dirty dishes and gotten them each a fresh beer.

His eyes went straight to the padded envelope in Chaz's hands and he snorted. "Honey, I can tell from here exactly what's in that."

"Yeah, I can pretty much figure it out too." After settling next to Andy, he set it down in his lap, picked up his beer and took a long drink. This was probably going to have to be his last drink tonight or he was going to be miserable tomorrow. He'd switch to water for the next round.

"You know what I just thought of?" Andy asked out of the blue.

"Oh, God help me." Chaz startled himself since he'd intended to just think that, not say it out loud. "I mean, what?"

"I can't wait until the next Alliance meeting. Both you and Justin are part of the campus QSA, but now you've upped the queer percentage. The straights are gonna be bummed."

Chaz had to smile at that. "Yeah, well, I have a feeling that I wasn't fooling anyone, not that I was trying to. Obviously the two of us are tight, and you patting my ass every time I walk by had to be a clue." He studied the package in his lap. "And I'm getting the impression that everyone already knew about Justin except for me."

"The spouse is always the last to know." Andy nodded his agreement. "I'm still looking forward to the first time you guys walk in holding hands."

Chaz studied Andy. "Did you know? About Justin, I mean."

Andy pressed his lips together, obviously trying to suppress a smile.

He smacked his friend on the shoulder. "Why didn't you say something to me? God, all those times I confided in you how I felt about him." He set down his beer and dropped his burning face into his hands. "I'm so embarrassed. Man, I'm an idiot."

"It was pretty ridiculous how dense both of you were, but I suppose sometimes when you've known someone as long as you two have each other, you sort of hold onto what you know to be true. And obviously since you two were kids, you weren't talking about what flavor of sex partner you like... Or the toppings." Andy squeezed his thigh and Chaz looked up. Instead of the smug expression he expected, Andy wore a gentler look. "And with all that, I don't blame either of you for not wanting to rock the boat or risk your friendship in case you made a move the other person didn't want."

"Yeah." That was true on his part, and probably even more so on Justin's. "So now what? It's going to be like starting from scratch when he gets home."

Andy looked at him like he was crazy. "Are you kidding me with this? Not hardly. You're best friends and know every other aspect of each other better than anyone else on earth. You have all of that history, all of that friendship as a base. Now you're just...adding another component. Quit psyching yourself out."

Chaz found himself confessing his worst fear, "I'm just afraid that while he's away for so long, he'll...come to his senses. Like, once he's away from me, he'll figure out I'm not all that and he'll find someone else."

Looking increasingly frustrated, Andy sighed. "Chaz, I'm not gonna lie. That's entirely possible. Does that mean I think it's gonna happen? No fucking way. I'd bet my very hot ass that absence will make his heart grow fonder. After all" — he tilted his head up as he delivered his final point — "that's what's happening with you, right?"

Chaz swallowed hard. "I miss him like crazy."

"I know, honey." Andy leaned forward and gave Chaz a hard hug. Then he stood and stretched before heading toward the front door.

Surprised, Chaz got up and followed him, holding the still unopened package Andy had been so interested in before. "You're going? But I haven't..." He waved it around.

"That's okay. I mostly just wanted to see if I could get you to share. I don't have to actually see it. I'm sure you'll probably want to put it to use, and you don't need me here for that. I'm going to head home and see if Hugh stops by later."

Chaz frowned then tossed the package onto the hall table before taking Andy's face in his hands. They gazed at each other for a minute before Chaz gave Andy a light kiss on the lips. "Come back if you need to talk. Even if it's late."

Andy nodded and opened the door. He walked the short distance to his own unlocked door and paused at the threshold. "Go on. Have a good time." He winked at Chaz, and if the wink wasn't as saucy as his usual, Chaz gave his friend the respect he deserved and pretended not to notice.

After making sure that Andy was safely inside his apartment, Chaz closed and locked his door. As if drawn by a magnet, his gaze went to the package on the table. Rather than the nervousness he'd felt the first couple of times he'd opened one of Justin's toys, all he felt now was anticipation.

Time for some fun.

Chapter Fourteen

Justin breathed deep for the first time in hours as he squeezed his way off the 'chicken bus' that he'd taken back into Antigua for his first time in the city since he'd gone out into the remote part of the country. He'd been in small, impoverished villages, in disheartening living conditions, working long days to help teach villagers to install the rooftop rain-gathering and filtration systems they were distributing to help provide a source of clean water by utilizing the precipitation that was so plentiful this time of year.

The experience had been equally frustrating and rewarding, but all in all enlightening. Never would he take his easy life for granted again. Only the randomness of birthplace kept him from being one of the people he was trying to help — the kids who seemed so small because they rarely had enough to eat, and the villages who were missing an entire generation of men due to the civil war that had torn the country apart.

He was glad he'd come — but he missed Charlie.

Late at night, often fighting to sleep despite his exhaustion, he thought of Charlie and wished that he could talk to him. His memories of him kept him going on the days when everything seemed to go wrong, and his dreams of their future gave purpose to his work.

Once he'd checked in at the organization's headquarters and retrieved the belongings he'd stored there — including his phone — he headed to the dormitory rooms and by habit, checked the triple bunk room he'd been in before. It was empty, so he went in and tossed his stuff down on one of the cots. Luke and Carlos were still on location – as friendly as they'd become, they'd agreed to take turns coming into the city for their halfway visit so that things didn't screech to a halt.

He was starving, tired and anxious to talk to Charlie, but first he was dying for a shower with soap. Justin snorted. Kind of ironic, since he'd been soaked for weeks. It was the middle of the rainy season here and he'd been working outside in it the entire time. But that was different from hopefully warmish water with soap. He ran his hand over his face – it was a full beard by now and definitely the most facial hair he'd ever had. Definitely needed a photo. Charlie would get a kick out of it, and Byron would definitely have a laugh.

Before he took his kit to the shower, he plugged in both of his phones – the new one to call Charlie from and his regular one to take some pictures, and also to get Byron's number from. The only phone numbers he had memorized were his family's and Charlie's. He probably wouldn't bother shaving, on second thought, at least not until after the second half of his trip – it would just grow back.

When he finally stripped off his clothes and looked down at himself in the cramped shower, he grimaced. Man, he'd lost a lot of weight. He had an obvious six-pack now, but he'd gotten it from slimming down rather than doing crunches.

He turned on the water just long enough to get his skin and hair wet then turned it off while he soaped up and worked shampoo into his hair. Conservation was ingrained by this time, and he knew he'd be changing his practices at home too. Once he'd rinsed off, he toweled dry then wrapped it around his waist. He shook his head at the reflection of his long-for-him hair and beard then brushed his teeth.

When he was back in his bedroom, he got dressed in cleanish clothes then checked his phones. After he snapped a few selfies on his normal one for when he got home, he looked up Byron's number then called him on the other one.

"Hello?"

"Hey, man."

"Justin? Wow. How are you? *Where* are you?"

He smiled and lay back on the cot. "Still in Guatemala—Antigua. I have a break for a couple days, so thought I'd give you a quick call."

"Feel like you've been gone forever. Good trip?"

"Yeah, definitely. Just…"

Byron chuckled. "You miss your guy. Haven't seen him around at all. How were things when you left?"

"Maybe not great since he wasn't talking to me, but we talked a few weeks ago and that went pretty good." Justin hoped that things were still good when he got around to calling him later on. It wasn't a lot of fun, having the situation so out of his control for so long, but he supposed that if they survived this, they'd get through anything.

"I'm glad, Just. It'd be great if you two could get on the same page. That would make things a lot fucking easier on everyone around you."

Justin had a feeling that most of Byron's sudden burst of vitriol wasn't aimed at him, but rather at the other Dog House boys.

"The two of them still tap dancing around each other?"

"It's driving me crazy. Something's going to come to a head here soon…in more ways than one."

They shared a laugh at that. God, it felt good to just joke around in his native language with someone who knew him well.

"How about you? Got your eyes on anyone?"

"Nope. I've no interest in tying myself down. And I'm not stupid, I'll definitely keep my options open—seen too many people find the right one to totally discount it—but no one I've come across so far. Shit, man, how much is this call costing you?"

"Not that much—it's more time that's at a premium right now."

"All right, I'll let you go then. Stay safe and have a good

trip. Let me know when you're back in town, okay? We'll get together. Maybe do another weekend out at the beach. Cody's wallet's still screaming from the last one, but a month from now I could probably talk him into it."

They said their goodbyes and Justin barely waited until the call had cleared before he was dialing Charlie. When he went to voicemail, he sighed and tried to figure out where he could be. "Hey, Charlie, it's me. I'm in Antigua for a couple of days. I'll try again later. Hope you're doing good. Bye." He cut himself off before he could babble on any more and start to repeat his crazy voicemail thing from last month.

Reality was, he was so out of touch at the moment that he wasn't sure what Charlie's schedule was this summer. Even if they had talked about it, it could have changed in the last month, and they'd had more important things to go over.

He considered that for a minute. The daily details of Charlie's life weren't any less important than the touch-feely stuff. He vowed to make sure that when they finally spoke, they did a little bit of catching up as well as talking about the 'fun stuff'.

Fatigue caught up with him and he turned onto his side. He'd try to reach Charlie again later. Right now a nap sounded like heaven.

* * * *

Justin jolted awake, disoriented for a moment, then realized that the phone right by his head was ringing. Still half asleep, he answered it by reflex.

"Hello?"

"Justin? Did I wake you up?"

"Charlie?" He sat up and looked around. Oh, wow. He was back at the headquarters. "Oh, let me call you back. Okay?"

"That's all right—"

"No. Seriously. Hang up. I'm hanging up now," he warned, though he still waited for a response.

"Fine. Hang up on me," Charlie snarked, but Justin could tell that he was smiling. "Bye."

"Bye." Justin quickly called back and it was answered almost immediately.

"Hey there."

"Hi." Justin lay back down and let Charlie's voice wash over him. He remembered his vow from earlier. "What have you been up to?"

"Me? You're the one who should be talking about what you're doing down there."

Justin smiled at how surprised Charlie had seemed by the question. "I'm interested. I was thinking about it earlier when I went to voicemail and I realized I really don't have any idea what your schedule is like."

"Oh. Not much. It's summer, you know?"

Charlie seemed reluctant to delve into the topic, but Justin persisted. "You working?"

"Just two day shifts—Tuesdays and Thursdays. Um... I'm TAing one section for Peterson on Monday afternoons, and have Monday and Wednesday morning classes."

Just learning the flow of Charlie's days settled something inside Justin that he hadn't known was bothering him. He could picture Charlie's days very clearly, having lived with him ever since they were freshmen, first in the dorms, then in their current apartment.

"Are you still shoving all of your studying and research into those days and vegging out in the apartment over the weekend?" he teased.

"Pretty much," Charlie admitted. "I did go to Andy's for dinner Saturday night... Well, we started at Andy's then we moved back over here when we ran out of wine." He huffed a laugh.

A slight pang of jealousy took Justin by surprise. "Oh? Late night?"

There was a pause before Charlie answered, "Not really.

What exactly are you asking?"

"Nothing. I'm glad you're having a good time with other people." And he was. He sighed and admitted, "That's just me missing doing stuff with you. Summers have always been fun for us."

"It's been hard for me too. I didn't realize how much we did together until..." Charlie paused for a few beats.

Justin knew what he meant so he went ahead and finished for him. "Until I wasn't there to drag you into the car barefoot?"

As he'd intended, Charlie burst into laughter. "Yeah, something like that. So tell me about what you've been doing there."

Justin told a few stories about his travels and some of the challenges he'd faced. It was definitely the Cliff's Notes version and they both knew that—they would have plenty of time for the details later on. They spoke for a while longer before Justin finally had to satisfy his curiosity and ask the question that had been on his mind for a long time.

"Have you opened everything yet?"

The temperature seemed to have gone up about ten degrees, and it was only after Justin had asked that question that Chaz realized it probably had. He was still sitting in his car, and since he'd turned off the car when he'd parked after coming home from campus, the warm weather and late afternoon sun were starting to bake the interior. He probably should have gone up to the apartment before calling Justin, but he'd listened to the voicemail as soon as he'd left the library, and with great effort he'd put off calling Justin back until he was done with the short drive home.

After he'd pulled into his assigned slot, he'd been unable to wait another moment before calling, hitting dial and fully intending to walk up to the apartment while they were speaking. He'd been a bit caught off guard when Justin had insisted on calling him back, so he'd sat there, not wanting to somehow miss the call, though that was pretty silly.

How many times had he answered the phone without any problems while walking across campus or moving from room to room? But sat he had, and after they'd started talking again, his plan to move inside had flown from his mind as he'd enjoyed the rare contact with Justin.

He rolled his eyes at himself and opened the door then answered Justin, "Not everything."

"Still trying to have patience? I'm impressed."

Chaz was pleased by his praise, but couldn't think of anything to say in response.

"Well, I'm glad you're enjoying the process, however you're pacing it."

"I..." Chaz cleared his throat. "I am. Enjoying it, I mean."

"Hmm." Justin's sexy hum put an ache in Chaz's chest. He quickly gathered his book bag as Justin continued, "I'm not sure if I should follow up by asking you what you've opened or why you're waiting to see what the rest are."

Chaz slammed the door shut and cleared his throat as he locked the door then walked toward the stairs, not sure what to say.

"Where are you at anyway?"

"Just walking up to the apartment. Sorry. Hold on a sec and I'll be inside." He hustled up the steps then held the phone to his ear with his shoulder as he unlocked the door in record time. He dropped the bag and kicked the door closed behind him. "Okay, I'm inside."

"You weren't on the phone while you were driving, were you?"

"No." Damn it. "I called you after I got to the complex, from the parking lot," he admitted.

"Well, I'm glad you're home now. Go ahead and take the time to get comfortable."

"That's okay." He managed to get his shoes off then went to sit on the couch. "I went casual today. It's pretty relaxed in the summer, you know?"

"So, what are you wearing?"

The stereotypical dirty phone call question made Chaz

laugh and he was pleased when Justin joined in. "Uh, khaki cargo shorts and a T-shirt," Charlie answered after an unnecessary but automatic glance down. "Very boring, I know."

"Nah. I can totally picture you. Well, except I don't know which T-shirt..." The way Justin trailed off made it clear that he expected Chaz to fill in the blank.

Oh crap.

Now Chaz was in a quandary because he was actually wearing one of Justin's tops. Never in his wildest dreams would he have thought that he'd be caught when Justin was over three thousand miles away. "Um..."

After a pause where Chaz was mentally scrambling for what to tell him, Justin cut into his thoughts, sounding surprised. "Um? Why 'um'? It's a pretty straightforward question...unless you're hiding something."

Chaz's face grew even warmer. Obviously it was way too late to try to come up with a plausible lie. "I'm wearing the Teva logo one," he admitted.

Silence hummed over the miles between them. "The one of mine that's so perfectly worn and comfortable that I left it at home because I didn't want to risk ruining or losing it down here?"

Nodding in confirmation even though there was nobody to see him, Chaz reluctantly confirmed, "That's the one."

Justin blew out a breath, and Chaz grimaced, ready to apologize.

"I love that you're wearing it, Charlie. That's pretty hot."

"It is?" he blurted then grimaced. Man, he wished he had a filter between brain and mouth. "I mean, you're not mad?"

"Of course I'm not mad. You can wear anything you want of mine. Well—the stuff that fits anyway." There was a burst of laughter over the line that made Charlie smile in response, then Justin explained, "I just had a vision of you trying to wear my jeans and them sliding right off your hips. That's pretty hot too. Comical, but hot. Sexy guy."

Charlie's mouth dropped open. Him, sexy?

There was a long pause where Justin could picture Chaz's blush rising from his neck to his cheeks. The patches that he always got were almost rectangular along his cheekbones, like the stripes athletes put on to cut the glare. But his favorite part was how Chaz's upper chest and neck reddened first. Always made him zero in on his collar area when he teased.

Before the embarrassment torpedoed the call altogether, he decided to let Chaz off the hook. "It felt so good to take a shower with soap and a little bit of warmth to it. I mean, it's so hot down here that you would think a cold shower would feel good, but it's a shock. I'm never going to take hot water heaters for granted again in my life."

The pace of the conversation picked up after that, and Justin thought he did a good job of not letting his jealousy come through when Chaz got around to talking about his concerns for Andy.

"It's just not like him to let some guy dictate what he does. He's just not the same." Chaz sighed. "I don't know what to say to him."

"Maybe they're just finding a place to come together. Relationships take compromise."

"Yeah, but it seems like Andy's doing all the compromising and Hugh is the one getting all the benefits. Then again, Andy's really into him. Gah!"

"He's a grown man, and very strong-willed from what I've seen. I know you worry about him, but honestly, I'm sure he'll be fine."

"I hope so. I never thought I'd see Andy so... I just think that a relationship that changes you so much your best friend barely recognizes you can't be good in the long run."

Justin couldn't help but notice the slight subtext running through the conversation. Take out the specifics and it might have been about the two of them. He decided to tackle the elephant in the room. "Does it bother you that I take the lead with us?"

"No!"

The speed of the reply couldn't be anything but genuine and Justin relaxed muscles he hadn't noticed had tensed.

"I mean, I'm very different than Andy. It's not anything close to the same situation. I'm... You..." Chaz coughed. "We've always been this way together. We're just...taking it to a different level?" He trailed off at the end as though asking for Justin to agree, which he was happy to do.

"You know that I've always wanted to care for you, for you to be happy. Best friends, right? That doesn't change. We're just—as you say—adding a different aspect to it. And if you trust me..."

"I do."

Justin smiled in relief at the sincerity and conviction in that answer. "Then there's no reason our change won't work just as well as our friendship has. But the friendship will always be my number one priority. If I ever think that something would damage that foundation or hurt you, I'll be the first to back off."

"I don't want you to. Really—"

"But I will if I have to. You always have a choice, too," Justin pointed out. He sensed Chaz's worry amping back up, and wanted to end on a good note. "I think we're on the right track, though."

"I think so too." Chaz's voice was deeper than usual. "And thanks for the reassurance with Andy. I know you two aren't exactly each other's biggest fan."

"We have you in common, so I'll try to get closer to him, for your sake. If he's willing."

"Now that would get me worried—if you two suddenly became best friends," Chaz joked.

Justin looked at the time and winced. "I'd better get going. I need some sleep." He was actually almost dozing by this time, between the comfortable mattress, being clean and hearing Chaz's voice.

"Okay. Get some sleep. I'll talk to you whenever you can."

"Goodnight," Justin murmured, already in that fuzzy zone that was half dreamy and half aware, still not wanting to say goodbye.

"Night, Just." Chaz's voice followed him down into a comforting darkness.

Chapter Fifteen

Chaz was clicking down through his inbox past junk mail and the occasional subscription email, and almost deleted the one without a subject from an email address he didn't recognize. Then the word *Justin* jumped out from the preview and he froze with his finger on the left click button.

Justin was due home tomorrow and he was so wired with anticipation that he was surprised that he could get anything done. Eagerly, he opened the short message, thinking it might be from Justin from a borrowed email.

Hello, Charlie. Justin can't call or email... Asked me to let you know he's okay but can't make his flight and will have to reschedule. Carlos

Chaz frowned and battled a queasy jolt to his stomach. Justin was 'okay'? What did that mean—had he been injured? Carlos rang a bell—Chaz struggled to remember, but thought he was one of the other guys in the same group as Justin. So not some official or from the organization.

Knowing that it was probably fruitless since if it was a team member, Carlos probably had as sporadic access to the Internet as Justin did, he nonetheless typed out a quick response.

Hi, Carlos, thanks for letting me know. What happened? Does Justin need me to do anything for him? Charlie

He briefly wondered if he should check in with Justin's family, then decided against it. They knew how to reach him if something happened, not that they would probably think to do so right away. Not unless it was really bad and they needed to get his belongings…

Stop it. It said he was okay.

He needed a distraction asap, so he closed down his laptop and tidied himself up, then walked across the landing to Andy's.

A couple of knocks didn't get any result, so Andy was either gone or…busy.

Frustrated, he returned to his apartment, changed his clothes and put on some running shoes. He wasn't a regular runner, but jogged a couple of times a week. Maybe the exercise would do him some good. At least he wouldn't be sitting around stewing in his worry and disappointment.

* * * *

Chaz was just about back at the apartment when a honk penetrated the music through his ear buds. He turned to see Andy waving at him as he drove past. He flipped a U-turn and pulled up next to him.

"Hey, looking good. Come on — hop in."

"I'm all gross and sweaty." When all Chaz got was an eyebrow in response, he caved. "Fine." He opened the door and gingerly climbed in. "Where are we going?"

"Lee's Kitchen. I ordered takeout. Want something? You can call it in." Andy handed his phone over and pulled away from the curb. "It's the last number dialed."

Chaz wasn't hungry but he knew he would be later, and there was pretty much nothing in the apartment. He'd planned to go to the grocery store tomorrow to stock up again before Justin got home…

He sighed deeply then hit the button to call. He ordered his usual then hung up and put the phone back on the console.

Andy didn't say a word until they'd pulled into the parking lot in front of the Chinese restaurant and parked. "I thought you'd be happier than this with your guy getting home tomorrow."

"He's not coming tomorrow."

"What? How come? Did you talk to him?"

Chaz explained about the email. "So I'm not sure what's going on, and it's really hard to get hold of him."

Andy glanced at the clock then opened his door to get out. "I'll be right back with the food, then we'll go home and talk. Just remember—the guy said he was okay. All right?"

Chaz nodded. He was holding on to that with a death grip.

Andy was back in record time and on the way home, Chaz finally realized that Andy was being uncharacteristically quiet and he didn't think it was all due to his worry over Justin.

"Are you okay? You're kinda quiet."

His friend pursed his lips and gave him a sideways glance. "I'm fine."

"Uh-oh." Chaz knew that Andy hated the response 'fine' and usually avoided using it. His opinion was that *fine* was what people said when they didn't really want to give you the real answer. "Hugh problems?"

"Not in the mood to talk about it. I need to split a bottle of wine first."

Fine with Chaz. "Deal."

When they got back to the apartments, Chaz broke off to go take a quick shower and get into fresh clothes. Out of habit he checked his phone and groaned when he saw a missed call from Justin. He should have been happy that Justin had been able to get in touch, even if he hadn't been able to answer.

"Hey, Charlie. I'm going to be a few days late getting home. Got stuck when a road washed out and had to…"

It fuzzed out for several seconds and Chaz squinted trying to hear…as though that did any good.

"…end of the week, but I'm going to try to get on stand-by. So, anyway" —a sigh— *"ready to be home and see you. I'll get there as soon as I can. Gotta go—I'll call you when I can. Bye."*

He hit redial without much hope and it went straight to voicemail. He hung up instead of leaving a message. Then he rolled his eyes at himself, dialed again and this time when the message option came on, he said, "Hey, Justin. Yeah, I got your message from Carlos and also your voicemail. Can't wait to see you and catch up and..." He was babbling. "Travel safe and see you soon. Bye."

After plugging his phone in on the nightstand, he slid open the top drawer to look at its contents — a habit of late. He'd opened all of Justin's packages and the presents were nicely arrayed in the drawer. The plugs were arranged in size order alongside the dildo. Leather ankle and wrist restraints gave off a heady scent. And the nipple clamps were still nestled in the small jeweler's box with the clear top. The last item was some sort of super lube — waterproof, toy safe and really expensive — he'd looked it up online. The reviews said it was great for shower sex...

Stripping as he headed toward the bathroom, Chaz shook his head. He couldn't wait until Justin was back and they didn't have to play phone tag ever again.

* * * *

His mood considerably improved between hearing Justin's voice and getting cleaned up, Chaz then turned his focus toward being a friend for Andy.

"Soooo...?" he drew out meaningfully. He upended the empty wine bottle and added a few drops to his still half full glass.

Andy grinned. "I love how you take everything I say so literally."

"Spill it."

"Okay, fine. Hugh and I are taking a break."

Chaz's jaw dropped. "Really? I'm not sure why that surprises me so much. You guys have been together for such a — "

"Not *together* together," Andy interrupted. "He'd have to

stop dating women for that to be the case."

"Oh." Chaz sobered. "I didn't know. Well, besides the blind date for the award thingy."

"This last one was pretty much the same thing. I wish…" Andy trailed off.

"Wish…?" Chaz prompted.

"Fuck. I wish he'd come out so they'd stop trying to fix him up with women."

Chaz patted Andy's thigh. "But he doesn't go out and try to find women to date, right? I mean, he's just being polite when they show up with some girl so he won't be…um, alone at stuff."

"Nice try." Andy slumped back against the armrest, lifting his feet to rest on Chaz's lap. He obligingly petted his lower legs and feet.

"I just don't think he swings that way. Not like Justin." And that was a worry of Chaz's. Maybe it shouldn't be, but he felt as though instead of competing with only half the adults in the world, he was competing with all of them.

Andy burst out laughing. "That boy is crazy about you. Has been for as long as I've known you two, and probably longer. I think now that your eyes are wide open—both of you—you don't have to worry about him going after some random chick."

"I could say the exact same thing about your situation," Chaz returned pointedly.

Andy took a deep breath, looked down at his hands then back up at Chaz. "Thanks. I needed to hear that." He sat up then knee-walked right over onto Chaz and gave him a tight hug that Chaz returned just as hard. "You rock."

"You too. So…" Andy disengaged and returned to his own end of the couch. "Since Justin will be home and completely monopolizing your time soon, let's watch a movie that he'd rather shoot himself than watch."

"Sounds great." Chaz wasn't sure any silly movie in the world would distract him from thinking about Justin, but Andy did have a point. Because once Justin got home, Chaz was never going to take their time together for granted.

Chapter Sixteen

Justin looked down at the phone in his hand, debating whether or not to call or text Charlie that he was back in the States. After a hopeful trip to the airport that afternoon, he'd managed to get a stand-by seat on today's flight to Miami, a day earlier than his rebooked flight. He stuffed it back into his pocket and waited for the aisles to clear so that he could stand. No, he'd wait until he knew whether he was able to get on the flight to the West Coast today, or if he was stuck in Miami until his flight tomorrow.

After he deplaned and went through customs, he headed straight to the airline's customer service counter. He was third in line and shifted back and forth impatiently, though it did feel good to stand. Finally it was his turn.

"How can I help you today?"

"I'm scheduled for a flight to Portland tomorrow and want to see if I can get there today."

The woman's drawn-on eyebrows rose skeptically but she began typing anyway. "I doubt there's anything today. With the time change and distance..." She squinted at the screen and shook her head. "Let me see your itinerary." She held out her hand and after a bit of fumbling in his pockets, he came up with his paperwork.

She typed some more, looking back and forth between the sheet and the screen. "See, even your original flight — or is that your rebooked flight? — had you overnight in Miami. And that's the only thing we could do today too. What I would recommend is staying in a hotel then trying to get on one of the first flights tomorrow."

Justin rubbed at his eyes with thumb and forefinger and

tried not to take his frustration out on her. "It's just that there was a landslide that took out the road in Guatemala so I missed my flight and I've been gone for two months... And I just really want to get home," he trailed off with a sigh.

To her credit, she did look sympathetic. "Would you feel better getting to LAX tonight? It'll be too late for a connection, but I'm sure you could get on an early flight home from there."

Closer would be better. He still felt like he was a world away.

At his nod, she began typing again and after what seemed like forever, the sound of printing came from under the counter. She slotted the boarding passes into his old envelope.

"Here. I've confirmed you on the LAX flight, and then the first connection to PDX in the morning."

"Confirmed...?" *Not standby?*

She smiled for the first time, revealing a gap. "Yes, you're booked and have seat assignments. I even gave you an exit row for extra leg room on the LAX flight."

He could've kissed her. "Thank you so much."

She nodded and pursed her lips. "Go on now. And have a nice day. Next person in line?"

Justin gave her a grin and winked, then grabbed his bag and let the couple behind him past. He had a few hours and since he didn't have to be there at the gate to pounce on the first gate attendant to try to get on the standby list anymore, he was going to find a sit down restaurant that served burgers and fries and beer. He'd call Charlie from there.

* * * *

The next morning, Justin paid the taxi driver and looked up at his apartment building. It was so strange being home — for some reason everything looked so different. His car and Charlie's were parked side by side in their assigned spots and he patted his as he went by.

In the end, he'd decided that it would be more fun to surprise Charlie, so he walked up the steps to the apartment then quietly unlocked the door. All was quiet. Either Charlie was gone somewhere he could walk to, or he was still asleep. Justin checked the time. Almost ten, so it was possible. The closed bedroom door at the end of the hall pointed to that being the case.

Not wanting to wake him up, Justin walked into his bedroom and set his bag by his closet, then unzipped it and pulled out an envelope he'd kept with him the whole trip. Twirling it in his hands, he debated about slipping it under Charlie's door, but it was probably too bulky to fit.

He tossed it on the neatly made bed. Hmm — *too* neatly made. Justin smiled thinking about Charlie sneaking in to grab T-shirts and maybe even use his bed.

Charlie was just down the hall sleeping, but he just couldn't force himself to walk in and wake him up. He'd be up soon anyway. And it was a beautiful day to be home. He'd make some coffee and go sit on the balcony overlooking the park.

It was about a half hour later when Justin thought he heard movement in the apartment. He leaned back in the chair, trying to see inside, but there was nothing out of the ordinary in the living room. He stood and stretched, still a bit stiff from three flights in twenty-four hours, then took his cup and walked inside. After putting the empty mug on the kitchen counter, he walked back to his bedroom...and began to grin like a fool.

The envelope had been opened and the T-shirt strips he'd used to tie up Charlie were scattered on the bed.

Smirking, he pulled his phone out.

After he'd dropped the swimsuit and strips of T-shirt on Justin's bed, Chaz had turned on his heel and retreated quickly to his own room, unwilling to face Justin yet if he was indeed back in the apartment. Especially while he was naked and aroused.

Now he paced, and a blush crept up his chest to his neck and face. He had gotten in the habit of walking around nude while he had the place to himself. What if Justin had come in on him?

He hurriedly stepped into a pair of gray sweat shorts, tugging them carelessly up to his hips, wincing as the elastic waistband briefly caught on his erection. Two months was a long time. What if some gorgeous Latin babe or hunk had caught Justin's eye? Or another volunteer on the team? Just because he had wanted to remind Chaz of their kinky interlude didn't mean that he still wanted anything more. Chaz frowned, rummaging for a T-shirt. The ring of his cell phone had him spinning around, his heart jumping into this throat.

Get a grip, he chastised himself. He quickly followed the ring tone across the room to snatch up the phone. His heart jackhammered even faster when he recognized Justin's cell number. He gulped a few quick breaths of air before answering.

"Hello?" Chaz was proud of his tone, casually inquiring and slightly bored.

"Did you find it?"

Chaz shuddered at the low caress of the sexy voice he hadn't heard this clearly in so long. "Uh, find what?" he attempted valiantly.

Silence. Chaz grimaced and gave in. "Oh, you mean the package." He swallowed with effort. "Yes," he admitted.

"And you opened it." This was not a question, but a statement. Chaz could almost hear the smile on the other end of the line. "You always were as curious as a cat."

"Well, it did have my name on it," Chaz muttered defensively, rubbing his scalp with his right hand as he sat on the bed.

"What were you doing in my room, Charlie?" This time Chaz could definitely hear the humor in Justin's voice, and he relaxed.

"Just fooling around," he teased back.

"Well, if you want to fool around, go back to my room."

"How do you know I'm not still in it?" Chaz challenged.

"Because I am."

Chaz dropped the phone from his nerveless fingers as the call disconnected. Two months of waiting and wondering had just come to an abrupt end. Suddenly not able to wait a moment longer to see Justin, he turned and strode down the hall, stopping in the bedroom doorway.

Justin stood by his bed, looking tanned and fit and darkly handsome, like a fallen angel. The uncertain look in his eyes took Chaz's breath away, and he didn't hesitate, but took the last couple of steps right into Justin's arms, holding him tight as if he would never let go. Justin closed his arms around him and pulled him along as he fell backwards into the bed. They sought each other gazes, and Chaz felt warmth and relief flow over him at the love and desire he saw, knowing that it was reflected in his own eyes.

His gaze, as always, dropped next to Justin's mouth, and he flushed a bit as he murmured, "We've never kissed."

Justin smiled tenderly. "We have a lot of things to look forward to. Right?" A small measure of the earlier uncertainty returned, tugging at his heart, and Chaz dropped his mouth to Justin's, rubbing lightly, then parting to invite a deeper kiss. He couldn't believe he finally had those beautiful lips under his own, and his cock instantly resumed its earlier rampant state of arousal as Justin stroked his tongue into Chaz, slicking along the inside of his lips, tangling with his tongue, tasting of mint and sexy man.

Meanwhile, Justin's hands were roaming over the thin barrier of Chaz's comfortable clothing, learning the lean musculature of his back and hips, then raking into his hair. "Your hair is so long," he observed contentedly. He tangled his hands in it and gave a light tug, and Chaz groaned in response. "You and your sensitive head." He drew Chaz's head back down, this time slanting over his lips and pressing demandingly as he took control of the kiss.

In a quick move, Justin flipped them over, thrusting one muscular thigh between Chaz's legs, then using both knees to kick his legs apart, lowering himself until their cocks aligned.

"Oh fuck." Chaz pressed upwards and their erections rubbed against each other through their clothing. They groaned in unison. Suddenly Chaz couldn't wait to be naked, and pushed against Justin's firm chest, trying to get free.

"No!" Justin growled, and nipped at his neck.

"Clothes. Off this time. Please," Chaz panted in explanation. He couldn't keep his hips still, thrusting up against Justin until he lifted himself off, prompting a contrary mutter of disappointment from Chaz.

"Clothes, Charlie," Justin reminded him, amused, pulling his shirt over his head and reaching for his belt buckle.

"Oh... Yeah," Chaz drawled, watching the show from beneath. "Wow, you're ripped."

Justin frowned at his roommate. "What about your clothes?"

Chaz smiled lazily, barely able to tear his eyes from Justin's sculpted chest. "I'm only wearing two things. You have much more work to do."

Justin gave him a grin that he felt down to his toes, then climbed off and gave the quickest strip show in history as he bared himself for his appreciative audience. He stood there for a moment with a crooked smile, and Chaz admired Justin's tanned torso and his muscular arms, even more developed than he remembered. His magnificently erect thick cock jutted above long, defined legs sprinkled with dark hair. As Chaz enjoyed the view, his erection managed to sneak out of the top of his loose shorts.

Justin shot him a look of pure lust as he reached for the waistband and made quick work of the shorts. His brow quirked. "I thought you said you were wearing two things."

Chaz fought his inevitable blush as he let his legs loll

apart, revealing the black base of the plug, and Justin went still. His cock jumped, and Chaz watched eagerly as precum welled from his slit. Like a man in a trance, Justin ran his hand down Chaz's leg, never taking his eyes off the intimate display. "You used them," he managed. "Have you enjoyed them?"

Chaz cleared his throat. "Yes."

"Tell me."

"I... They felt good going in." Justin slowly nodded for him to continue and kept up the stroking of his inner thighs, migrating closer to the top with each pass. "I pretended they were you," he confessed daringly in a whisper, and Justin closed his eyes for a moment and shuddered.

His response gave Chaz confidence. "I wore them out in public sometimes, and nobody knew but me." Chaz clenched his muscles as Justin lightly brushed his sac, then nudged the plug with a finger, causing it to shift within his passage. "Oh God."

"What about jacking off?" Justin trailed his fingers up Chaz's erection, following a vein to the tip, then encircling the head.

"Umm, yes, but I haven't finished."

"For how long?"

"Since you left in June."

Chapter Seventeen

That caught Justin's full attention, drawing him away from his play, and he crawled deliberately up Charlie's body until they were face to blushing face. "You haven't come since I left?" he asked incredulously. "Why?"

"Well, what you said about not coming without permission — that night at the beach house? — kind of stayed in my head, I guess, even though we didn't talk about it specifically. The thing is, I *have* tried a few times." He kept his eyes averted as he confessed. "But I haven't been able to go all the way."

He couldn't believe what he was hearing, but the fact that Charlie had taken what he'd said so much to heart pleased the Dom in Justin. "You haven't gotten your rocks off once in two months?" Justin demanded intently.

"No — I mean, yes. Quite a few times. But just... Well, in my sleep," he confessed. "Not by my own hand."

That conjured an image in Justin's head of another man — Andy — stroking Charlie's cock. He clenched his jaw. "And anyone else's hand?" he gritted out, hating his reaction but he'd had a long time to think and picture Charlie here alone with Andy across the hall.

Charlie paled, evidently startled by the unexpected display of jealousy. "No, of course not!"

He ran his hands along Justin's jawline, and Justin tried hard to relax back into his previously seductive mood.

"Justin," Charlie added soberly, shaking his head. "You have to be able to trust me."

Justin took a deep breath and rested his cheek against his temple. "I do trust you. I'm sorry. It's been driving me crazy thinking about you here with your flirty friend right next door, and me not here." He looked up ruefully. "I'm trying not to be a Neanderthal about this. I sound like a possessive jerk. But I really feel like you're mine. My friend, my roomie, my...lover. Mine." Justin punctuated each *my* with a light brush of lips on Charlie's mouth. By the final word, his lips were fully on Charlie's in a firm, coaxing kiss that fanned their desire into something urgent and hot. "I need to be in you." Justin gazed down at Charlie, wanting the decision to be his.

Chaz nodded and drew him back in for another tender kiss before reaching for the plug.

"No, let me." Justin brushed his hand away and began laying a trail of fire down his body, stopping to tease his nipples into hard nubs before pulling at them with his teeth, then continuing to mouth and lick his way down his chest to brush past his belly to swiftly engulf his swollen cock in the moist depths of his mouth. Chaz nearly succumbed to the incredible heat suddenly surrounding him. Justin explored the head with his tongue, flicking under the sensitive edge, then pushed his lips down the shaft, drawing out the suction on the way back up.

Chaz was already dizzy with the need to come. Justin cupped his balls in his large, warm hand, running his nose over the sac as if to drink in his scent, then gently taking first one, then the other into his mouth. He raised his eyes to meet Chaz's gaze, and he grasped the end of the plug, inciting a drawn-out moan from low in his throat as he pulled it almost all the way out before slowly reinserting it, keeping eye contact all the while.

Justin smiled a hot smile as he continued to work the thick plug in and out, and just when Chaz thought he couldn't help but spill over the edge, Justin stopped and reached for the bedside table drawer. He pulled the plug all the way out then paused for a moment to rip open and slowly ease on a condom before lowering his head for a brief, hard kiss.

Adding some lube to his fingers, Justin made quick work of lubing the condom, then entered Chaz with two slick fingers. Chaz gasped at the intimate touch, so warm and different from the plugs he had been using. Slowly adding more lube, Justin patiently worked his hole, turning his fingers then thrusting deep. His sharp eyes held Chaz pinned as he crooked up and deliberately grazed his prostate again and again until Chaz couldn't help squirming and grabbing his own cock, thrusting into his hand in accompaniment to Justin's movements.

"God, Justin, will you please just fuck me already?" he begged, his voice strained.

Justin raised an eyebrow at his impatience, but didn't take him to task, immediately acquiescing and placing the blunt tip of his cock at the prepared entrance, bracing his body above him. "I like this. I want to watch your face as I take you. As we become one." It sounded like a benediction as he began to push inside, and Chaz felt himself yielding to the insistent pressure. "Pull your legs back, baby. C'mon, let me in." The head popped past the tight ring, and Justin paused as Chaz stopped breathing. The initial burn quickly turned to an amazing fullness that he wanted so much more of.

Justin bent down and kissed him, waiting until Chaz just couldn't be still any longer and thrust his hips upward in a silent plea. Justin responded instantly, pressing forward in a smooth motion until he bottomed out.

"Okay?" he asked, and Chaz could only nod, breathless with the sensation of being utterly possessed by the man he had loved for so long. Chaz undulated his hips and Justin groaned, then set a steady pace, rocking slowly in and out. "Charlie."

"Fuck me," Chaz invited in a hoarse voice. "So close."

"Give it to me, then." And Justin snapped his hips and slammed into Chaz full length, pressing and holding for a long moment, then hitting him once more, twice.

"Justin!" he shouted as his passage tightened, constricting

around Justin's thick shaft, followed by ribbons of his pearly cum splashing on his chest. His vision blurred and his eyes drifted closed, then popped open as Justin flexed once more and poured himself into Chaz, filling him with hot seed as the intensity and love on his face took Chaz's breath away.

"Charlie, Charlie," he groaned as he dropped over him, cupping his head in his hands as he rested his forehead on Chaz's. He kissed him once, twice, butterfly kisses mingled with the warmth of his breath. His thumbs brushed at Chaz's temples. All the while, those brilliant blue eyes never left his own.

"I love you, Charlie."

Chaz felt overwhelmed as the little bubble of hope that had begun two months ago burst over him in a wash of love and rightness. "I love you too, Justin. I always have."

Justin lightly butted their foreheads together then lifted to kiss the spot. "Mine?"

"Yours," Chaz agreed. "Forever." That earned him a smile that turned into a grin when Chaz quickly added, "As long as you return the favor."

Justin's eyes twinkled down at him. "Okay. Each other's forever." That sexy quirk of his brow. "So, any other favors I should be doing for you?"

"Yeah. Teach me." Chaz watched those bright eyes darken in delightful response as he raised his hand into view, holding one of the T-shirt strips. "Welcome home, Justin."

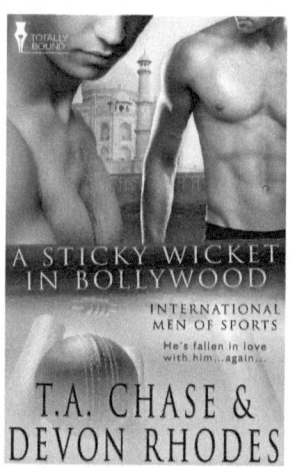

A Sticky Wicket in Bollywood

Excerpt

Chapter One

The noise hit Rajan like a wave crashing over him as soon as the doors to the chauffeured car were opened. His agent, Beni Sharma, was the first to exit and the flashes from the waiting cameras lit up the interior momentarily before the photographers evidently realised that Sharma wasn't the main attraction.

Rajan took a breath, glad for even a moment's respite from the badgering. He needed a break. He'd been filming non-stop for close to a year, and the exhaustion had finally caught up with him. He'd lost nearly ten kilos for his last role, since they'd needed a lot of beach shots and required even more muscle definition than his natural weight allowed for. Starvation and intense workouts had cut his physique, but had left his already low reserves seriously depleted.

Sharma, however, refused to hear him when he spoke about needing some time off, and had been trying for days to get him to commit to yet another 'must-do' project. And he wasn't taking no for an answer.

Rajan received a not-so-gentle nudge to the shoulder.

"Are you ever going to get out? Wait...how do I look?"

He turned back to look at his girlfriend Karishma Saxena, one of the rising stars of Bollywood, according to the infatuated media. It was her premiere-he was merely her escort this evening, as he hadn't been in this production.

He obediently ran his gaze over her, from head to...well... cleavage.

"How does that dress even stay up?" he asked. It was gold and sparkly and looked as though, with any sudden move, gravity would make sure she had front page coverage in all the wrong kinds of magazines.

She raised an eyebrow. "Double-sided tape and wishful thinking. Now, seriously..."

"You look beautiful, as always," he answered honestly. It wasn't her fault he wanted to be anywhere but here. Anywhere far away from the madness waiting outside the door.

He turned back to the open door and began to step out. As he did, he could tell the moment they recognised him.

"Rajan! Rajan Malik! Are you with Karishma?"

"Rajan! Look this way!"

He pasted a smile on and straightened. This time the flashes were almost blinding. He immediately turned to reach out to Karishma, assisting her to step out onto the red carpet, then offering his arm as they faced the wall of cameras and shouting reporters.

The usual questions were called out-asking about their next projects, who they were wearing, and the latest favourite...

"When is the wedding?"

Beni Sharma represented both Raj and Karishma and,

after allowing a minute or so of photographs, he moved into the tableau and posed next to them.

"Now, now," he pandered. "These two won't have time for a wedding until after they wrap up filming on the new movie they're co-starring in."

It took all the professionalism Rajan had to maintain his smile in the face of that deliberate bombshell. Fed up and about ready to create a scene, he put himself and Karishma in motion, walking slowly away from the car-and Sharma-along the red carpet leading towards the suburban Mumbai studio where the premiere was being held. He paused, as was expected, just under the awning, in front of the logoed background for more photographs. This is where Karishma and he would wait for her co-star for this film to arrive for even more pictures. As pissed off as he was at that moment, Rajan just didn't have it in him to buck tradition, though he wished he had the balls to just keep walking into the studio and find a quiet corner somewhere.

Maybe even watch the movie.

Rajan let Karishma subtly arrange them so he was standing slightly behind her. He knew his black suit with silver stripes and black shirt and tie would set off her gold and bright pink gown. They'd practised the pose they'd been coached on in front of the mirror after being dressed earlier. Seemed like almost every detail of his life was planned by someone else.

How the hell am I going to get out of this now?

Did he really even have a choice but to make the movie? Sharma had basically announced his participation, which would be faithfully reported to millions of people, including the principles of the studio. And they were determined to get him on board. He and Karishma had somehow become the couple to watch in Bollywood. So much so that the studio had booted the originally cast male lead last week under some contrived circumstances then had demanded, through Beni, to sign Rajan as his replacement.

It meant huge publicity...and a huge payoff. The contract

he'd been offered was enough to stun him. He'd finally made it to the A-list with this one.

He blinked, and it took some effort to reopen his eyelids all the way.

Yeah, a fat lot of good that'll do you if you're dead from exhaustion.

More books from Devon Rhodes

Pascal might be chasing the title of King of the Mountains, but will he realise in time that Laurent is chasing him?

It's well worth sacrificing his favorite T-shirt to try to save their relationship.

DEVON
RHODES

He's plotting
something
naughty...

GRAD SCHOOL GUYS

NAUGHTY
BY NIGHT

Normally, finding the hot neighbor in bed with your boyfriend would be the end — not the beginning — of a wonderful relationship.

The road to love is never smooth.

About the Author

Devon Rhodes

Devon started reading and writing at an early age and never looked back. At 39 and holding, Devon finally figured out the best way to channel her midlife crisis was to morph from mild-mannered stay-at-home mom to erotic romance writer. She lives in Oregon with her family, who are (mostly) understanding of all the time she spends on her laptop, aka the black hole.

Devon Rhodes loves to hear from readers. You can find contact information, website details and an author profile page at https://www.pride-publishing.com/